HIGH SCHOOL BITES

The Lucy Chronicles

LIZA CONRAD

nal
JAM
books

NAL Jam

Published by New American Library, a division of
Penguin Group (USA) Inc., 375 Hudson Street, New York, New York 10014, USA
Penguin Group (Canada), 90 Eglinton Avenue East, Suite 700, Toronto, Ontario M4P 2Y3,
Canada (a division of Pearson Penguin Canada Inc.) • Penguin Books Ltd., 80 Strand,
London WC2R 0RL, England • Penguin Ireland, 25 St. Stephen's Green, Dublin 2,
Ireland (a division of Penguin Books Ltd.) • Penguin Group (Australia), 250 Camberwell
Road, Camberwell, Victoria 3124, Australia (a division of Pearson Australia Group Pty.
Ltd.) • Penguin Books India Pvt. Ltd., 11 Community Centre, Panchsheel Park, New
Delhi - 110 017, India • Penguin Group (NZ), cnr Airborne and Rosedale Roads,
Albany, Auckland 1310, New Zealand (a division of Pearson New Zealand Ltd.)
Penguin Books (South Africa) (Pty.) Ltd., 24 Sturdee Avenue,
Rosebank, Johannesburg 2196, South Africa

Penguin Books Ltd., Registered Offices:
80 Strand, London WC2R 0RL, England

Published by NAL JAM, an imprint of New American Library,
a division of Penguin Group (USA) Inc.

First Printing, January 2006
1 3 5 7 9 10 8 6 4 2

NAL JAM and logo are trademarks of Penguin Group (USA) Inc.

LIBRARY OF CONGRESS CATALOGING-IN-PUBLICATION DATA

Conrad, Liza.
High school bites : the revolution starts now / Liza Conrad.
p. cm.
Summary: Having learned on her sixteenth birthday that Count Dracula exists and lives in
her hometown of Seattle, Lucy tries to save herself and her friends while wondering whether
her boyfriend is also a vampire.
ISBN 0-451-21752-7
[1. Vampires—Fiction. 2. High schools—Fiction. 3. Schools—Fiction. 4. Seattle
(Wash.)—Fiction.] I. Title.
PZ7.C764744Hig 2006
[Fic]—dc22   2005023674

Set in Sabon • Designed by Elke Sigal

Printed in the United States of America

Dedicated to
Alexa, Nicholas, Isabella, and Jack

Acknowledgments

A huge thank you to my editor, Anne Bohner, who never forgot that this book was a dream of mine, and who found a place for it at JAM. I love the JAM line—and a great big dose of appreciation to everyone from marketing to cover design.

Thank you to my agent, Jay Poynor. I know you're a "teeny little bit" old for teen lit—but you still get my concepts and support me.

An acknowledgment to my bestest pal, Pam Morrell, who, like Lucy and Mina, will stick together with me through anything.

To my family . . . especially little Jack, who brought a breath of fresh air and magic into our lives. And to the usual suspects—those pals who always gather 'round me and offer support and encouragement and friendship. You all know who you are.

To my dad, who always let me watch the "Creature Feature" and Dracula and Frankenstein movies when I was a kid.

And finally, to J.D. I'd starve to death without your cooking.

Prologue

S o . . . do you think the school will make me give
back the tiara?" I asked my best friend, Mina.

She stared at me. My dress was torn, I had blood-
stains on my homecoming queen sash, and I had broken a heel on my brand-new, to-die-for shoes. My
tiara dangled off to the side of my head, and my curls,
normally uncooperative in the rainy Seattle weather
anyway, had exploded. I looked like a Chia Pet.

"Lucy . . ." Mina said. "If I were Principal
Becker I wouldn't even let you come back to school
on Monday. You'll be in detention for the rest of
high school. Maybe even for the rest of your life."

"But it wasn't my fault." We stood surveying the
wreckage of the homecoming dance. The glass
punch bowl was in shards on the floor, and the huge
banner proclaiming the night of Pacific Cedar High's
homecoming dance was shredded to tatters.

"No, it wasn't your fault," Mina said. "Not exactly."

I looked at her. Her beautiful auburn hair—sort

of the color of a Canadian maple leaf—that she paid forty-five dollars to have styled in a fancy updo was a mess. She had a smudge of blood on her cheek, and her ivory satin slip dress had orange sherbet punch all the way down the front of it. Mascara was smeared around her pale green eyes.

I snapped, "What do you mean, 'not exactly'?"

"Well . . ." she said slowly. "You might have waited until *after* the last dance to pick a fight with Vic."

"Maybe," I said. "But if we're looking for someone to blame, I think you have to admit that it's Mr. Dobbs's fault."

She scrunched her mouth up and finally nodded. "Yeah. He did sort of start all this."

"Absolutely." It had all begun with Mr. Dobbs's English class. Before his class, I'd never even thought about vampires. Or Transylvania. Or Dublin, Ireland. Or Bram Stoker. Or even crosses and holy water and garlic.

Nope. I was an ordinary sophomore in Seattle, worried about SATs, bad-hair days, and water retention when I had PMS.

And now?

Now I had to sleep with a crucifix.

I t's bad enough being fifteen. In fact, most days being fifteen is about all I can handle. Homework; Mrs. Ruthen, a.k.a. Mrs. Ruthless, the meanest teacher at Pacific Cedar High—perhaps even the world as we know it; my sometime-boyfriend, Vic; trying to get in driving practice on my learner's permit; my unmanageable hair in the rainiest state in the U.S.; and flat-chested to top it all off. What adult idiot said your four years in high school are the best years of your life?

And yet, all of that, including that I was this close to flunking Mrs. Ruthless's class . . . well, none of it compared to having to live with my father. I love him with all my heart, but he was bad enough when I was in kindergarten and elementary school. Now that my sixteenth birthday was just around the corner, he'd gotten more insane. And it's not like I'm exaggerating. My two best friends concur: "Lucy, you win the Weird Family of the Year award." Hands down. In fact, were there truly a

Weird Family contest, I would be wearing the winning tiara. And a sash.

✳

"Lucy, can you please work out your algebra equation from homework question two on the blackboard?"

I swear, Mrs. Ruthless just looks out over that classroom, and when she sees someone struggling she asks them up to the board for a little public humiliation. The D-plus on my report card already sucked, but did I really have to demonstrate my complete, pathetic stupidity when it comes to "If a equals b and b equals c, times the square root of 442, what's the answer"?

Mrs. Ruthless stared at me with those beady hamster eyes of hers. She had her usual expression on her face that said, *I hate all students and I am about to make your life a living hell.*

My best friends, Mark and Mina, sit next to me in Ruthless's class. Mark is a genius when it comes to math, so he helps me out with Ruthless, and I help him in English. When he writes he seems to forget that you need commas and periods. He writes how he talks. No breaths in between words.

As I stood to go to Ruthless's blackboard, Mark slipped me the answer on a small piece of paper just as I started down the aisle of desks. He winked at me, and I thought I was home-free. Mina smiled and gave me a thumbs-up.

"Lucy, what do you have in your hand?" Ruthless intoned.

"Nothing."

"I saw Mark give you a note, young lady." Yeah, of course she saw me. She's a satanic old woman with hidden devil's eyes in the back of her head. All right, I have no proof of that. But if I could, I'd search for the numbers 666 on her head somewhere.

Did I mention Mark is Pacific Cedar High's resident cartoonist for the yearbook and school newspaper? Because not *only* had he handed me the note explaining the vagaries of the proof I had to solve, he'd drawn a cartoon of Mrs. Ruthless riding a broomstick. So I found myself, a mere twenty-seven days into the new school year, sitting in the principal's office with Mark.

Principal Becker held the note in his hand and leaned back in his overstuffed fake-leather chair.

"Lucy . . . I'm not surprised to see you here, but Mark . . . I expect so much better from you."

"Thanks a lot," I snapped.

Mark looked over at me. I've known him for so long, I don't think I can even recall a memory that doesn't have him in it. His older brother, Tom, delights in tormenting us by reminding anyone within earshot that Mark and I used to take baths together when we were three. That was before my mother died. I barely remember her. Sometimes, though, I *do* remember Mark and me playing with bright-colored plastic sailboats in the tub.

"Lucy had nothing to do with this, Mr. Becker. I handed her the note. She shouldn't be punished," Mark said, running his hand through his hair. Not that there was much hair to do so. His mom cuts his entire family's hair (there are nine kids in his family) to save money, so Mark usually has a crew cut, often with a small bald patch where Mrs. Carnahan got a little too zealous with the clippers.

Mr. Becker stared at us from across the desk. "Lucy could have refused the note, or she could have told Mrs. Ruthen you were about to engage in cheating."

I tried to avoid rolling my eyes, and Mark gave me a look that said, *Yeah, right, what high school kid rats out a friend?*

"Mark . . . you may leave. You can serve detention every day until Friday."

Mark nodded. He doesn't mind detention. It beats fighting for the lone bathroom at home or studying in the room he shares with two of his brothers, including Jimmy, who is in that prepuberty stage when boys don't want to bathe very often.

I stood to leave with Mark. Mr. Becker said, "Not you, Lucy. We have to talk."

I sank back down in the chair. Mark shot me a sympathetic look as he left.

"Lucy . . . I called your father about this little incident and asked him to come to school. Do you know what he said?"

I nodded. It was the same answer anytime we talked about leaving the house. No.

"Your father refused. Said we could deal with it over the telephone. And Lucy . . . I've driven past your house. . . . It's on my way home each day."

"Why? Are you stalking me?" I tried to make a joke.

"No." he smiled. "Lucy . . . all I'm saying, I suppose, is that maybe you might want to talk to the school psychologist or one of the guidance counselors."

I shook my head. "I wouldn't know what to say."

"You don't think it's worth a shot?"

I shrugged. Mr. Becker opened and reached into his top desk drawer and pulled out a card. "Here, Lucy. It has the number of Carolyn Harris, the school psychologist. You could talk to her anytime you wanted."

He meant well, so I thanked him and stuck the card in my back pocket. The bell rang, signaling seventh period. "I have to go," I said.

"Okay, Lucy. But I want a progress report next week. And you can go to detention with Mark. No more artwork on Mrs. Ruthen, okay?"

I nodded. Then I left his office.

Sure . . . like I could walk into Ms. Harris's office—with homemade cross-stitched sayings in frames on the wall, like, "Believe in yourself"—and tell her the truth.

That my father hadn't left the house in ten years. That I needed an entire key ring—like the school janitors carry—in order to open all the locks he had on the house. What was I supposed to say? That my father was afraid? Of everything?

Chapter 2

With nine children, there was no way Mark would *ever* get use of the family car. He had way too many siblings with seniority over him, and with nine kids to feed, his mother had to work her budget with the efficiency of an accountant and the creativity of a genius. I mean, how many different ways are there to cook leftovers? So the Carnahans' getting another car was out of the question. He'll be walking until college. Until after college.

I didn't have my license yet, so that meant Mark and I walked home from school together. We could have ridden the bus, but there was this whole image thing—the bus is for the babies, the freshmen who don't have cars and can't drive. Walking was better than the bus—at least we could stop for a burger when we wanted, and we could talk. We also got rained on a lot—because we live in Seattle—but after a while you get used to not ever seeing the sunshine.

Supposedly Vic, who was sort of my boyfriend, was getting a car for his birthday. His parents seemed to have loads of money. He wouldn't just be getting *any* car, but a little MINI Cooper, which would just enhance his "coolness" factor. I expected Debbie McGovern to try to sink her claws into him the second he started driving his own car—though she barely gave Vic the time of day now. The walk home was three miles of suburbia. Neat, lush lawns (the rain is good for something) with trimmed hedges, tall cedars, and even a picket fence or two.

"Want to study at my house?" I asked Mark. He was one of the few people who found my father's eccentricities somewhat fascinating.

"Sure. Um . . . you think Mina will call us later?"

"Mina has her cell phone surgically attached to her ear. She'll call when she gets back from rehearsal." Mina was in the class play—the lead, as always.

I looked at Mark. Lately he had Mina on the brain.

We rounded the block toward home, and there it stood. Among brick ranches and prettily painted Cape Cod houses with dormer windows was my house, which looked like the Munsters or the Addams family lived there. At Halloween time, we were the house where the kids were too afraid to come to the door. I liked giving out candy to the kids, so I usually sat out on the sidewalk with a big bucket of Snickers bars and Tootsie Roll Pops and doled them out. That way the kids didn't have to go up to our doorbell.

Mark and I walked up the front path. Grasses and weedy-looking wildflowers grew tall. Dad didn't mow the lawn. Every once in a while he paid Mark thirty bucks to whack it all down short—sort of like a Mrs. Carnahan haircut—but Dad usually let it go.

We climbed the wooden front steps. Each one creaked and groaned. I took out my key ring and started unlocking locks. I used to get really frustrated doing it, until I got the brilliant idea to color-code the keys and locks with nail polish. Now I match the shade of the lock with the shade of the key. The main lock is Cherry Rocking Red.

I got the heavy wooden door open, and Mark and I walked in.

"Dad? I'm home. Dad?"

"In my study, Luce."

Mark and I walked through the living room to my father's study. He sat there, glasses perched on the bridge of his nose, poring over old manuscripts. He's a professor of medieval studies and ancient languages, but he stopped teaching after my mother died, and now he supports us by writing books, and also from a trust fund passed down from my mother's side of the family. Despite the fact that the outside of our house had weird turrets, a few honest-to-God gargoyles, and an overgrown garden, inside was the hushed velvet whispers of antiques my father and mother had collected on their travels before she got sick and he got crazy.

"Hi, Mr. Hellenberg."

"Hi, Mark. Studying today?"

Mark nodded. Mark and I studied together a lot. A scholarship was just about the only way for a Carnahan kid to go to college. He had two older sisters who went on soccer scholarships, and an older brother who would likely get a basketball one. The athletic gene skipped Mark. It would have to be based on his brains.

"What are you working on?" Mark asked my dad. My father, always somewhat secretive, closed the book he was reading. "Oh . . . nothing. Just old gibberish you kids wouldn't be interested in."

Interested? We wouldn't be able to *read* it unless we knew Latin or Greek, or Hungarian, which neither Mark nor I did.

I looked at the cover of the book. It had a monster on the front of it, a devil or something. Then I looked around the top of his desk, cluttered three inches thick with papers. The remnants of a sandwich I'd made for him the day before sat on a plate. Half a cup of coffee, clearly cold. "Did you eat anything today, Dad?"

He turned to look at me, and he suddenly had an expression of realization. "Um, no," he said sheepishly. "I hadn't even thought to stop and eat."

"I'll make you something," I said, and signaled Mark. We went into the kitchen together.

"How does your dad forget to eat?" Mark asked. I pulled cold cuts out of the refrigerator and started to make Dad a sandwich. Mark opened a bag of Doritos and dug in. I don't think Mark went more than two hours without eating, let alone a whole day.

As I slathered mayo on a slice of bread, I shrugged. "He's got Einstein syndrome."

"What's that?"

"He's almost too smart, so he doesn't think about things you and I think about. He's on another planet, and we missed the space shuttle to it. You know . . . Einstein had, like, thirty identical black suits, black socks, and white shirts. He didn't want to have to waste a single brain cell thinking about what to wear. Dad? He can't be bothered with food."

"Weird."

"Tell me about it."

When I was little, we had a very nice house-keeper, whom I called Nana Marie. For some reason she didn't seem to mind the extra locks, the fact that my father never left the house, and all the rest of it. She had the room opposite mine. About two years ago a bout of pneumonia had weakened her, and we found her an apartment in a retirement community. Since then, Dad and I haven't eaten as well as we used to. I'm not really a very good cook. Macaroni and cheese is about the extent of my repertoire.

While Mark ravenously ate his Doritos—not having to share the bag with eight other brothers and sisters is a novelty—I went to the study and brought Dad his sandwich. He was standing next to his drafting table. Dad kissed the top of my head absentmindedly while scribbling in a notebook. He even writes in Latin. I could see he had drawn a picture of a monster-looking thing in black ink on one of the pages.

"What's that?" I pointed.

"Oh, nothing. Based on some old research."

He looked over at me. He wore horn-rimmed glasses—which he was always losing, leaving them anywhere from inside the refrigerator to next to the cat bowl when he fed Professor V, our very fat, very old black cat. Dad talked to him all day when I was in school—and even when I was home. He would ask the cat's opinion, like, "Don't you agree, Professor V?" And then our cat would meow. Dad had sandy blond hair and pale blue eyes that always looked a little sad, except when he was reminiscing about my mom or talking about me. He was kind of sentimental that way. He sometimes forgot to shave—like today—and when he did, his beard was white in spots. And he always wore the same thing—charcoal-gray pants, white shirt à la Einstein, with the sleeves rolled up, a plain gold crucifix my mother gave him, and Top-Siders. In the winter he had this hideous gray sweater with little moth holes in it, but he said someone once made it for him and it brought him good luck. Whatever.

"That thing looks scary," I said, pointing at the pen-and-ink drawing.

He stood very still. "It is. I'll explain all my research to you on your sixteenth birthday. I suppose I can't keep you a little girl forever. I can't believe that's one week away. Sixteen. Makes me feel . . . old."

"You're not old, Dad. Weird . . . but not old."

He smiled and sat down and started scribbling some more. *Someday,* I thought, *I'm going to have to learn Latin.*

That night I kept tossing and turning. I slept, but it seemed like every twenty minutes or so I'd wake up and stare at my digital clock, which would just remind me that in a mere few hours it would be blaring that it was time for school. I hate the mornings, and even drinking two cups of the coffee Seattle is famous for, I just can't stand the day before noon.

The house was creaking. A lot. After living here my whole life, I guess I'm so used to it, it's not scary. It's got hardwood floors and thick plaster walls, and it's just old, period. When Mark's grandmother came to stay with his family for a few weeks after his grandfather died, Mark stayed in one of our spare bedrooms—and most of the time ended up in a sleeping bag in my room. The noises the house made would creep him out all night long.

But that night, I don't know . . . I just couldn't sleep. It was as if the house were trying to tell me something. Actually, if I thought about it, it was a few weeks since I'd really slept soundly. I would wake up with some vague nightmare, something I couldn't remember.

Then I heard it. A cross between a tapping on my window and a scraping sound. I looked to my window and thought I saw a face. A man's face—handsome, with these really intense eyes that glowed. And it was as if he could speak to me. Not out loud, but in my head.

It's time, Lucy.

My heart pounded, and I flicked on my light, grabbed my phone to call 911 if I had to, picked up the nearest heavy thing I had—which happened to be my algebra textbook—and crept closer to the window. The glare from the light meant I couldn't see well, so I got closer to the window, my heart pounding so loud it was like there was a train in my chest. A heavy fog had descended on the backyard. I couldn't see anything—or anyone.

It's time, Lucy.

I shook my head to chase the voice away. I had to have dreamed it. I put my hated math book down, and I put the phone back on its base.

I told myself it was a dream. That was all. It had to be. Even though that face seemed so familiar. Those eyes. But I was really, really glad I hadn't called 911. I could just imagine what would have happened if they sent a squad car to my house.

Because, creepy fog and creepy noises aside, even a rookie cop would have pointed out something very, very obvious.

My bedroom is *way* up on the second floor, and just below it is a huge rosebush hedge with thorns so sharp they'd tear anyone to shreds.

There was no way anyone was at my window.

But just to be sure, I slept with my light on.

Chapter 3

For my sixteenth birthday, which fell on a Thursday, Vic handed me a card and asked me to go to dinner.

"I can't. I promised my dad I'd have dinner with him tonight."

"Tomorrow then?" Vic stared at me intently. He has a very heavy-duty stare, with these blue eyes that are almost the color of a glacier, which I and most of the female student population of Pacific Cedar High find very hot.

I nodded and shut my locker.

"I got you a cool present."

I felt my cheeks blush. Pretty much every time Vic was near me, I'd turn red. Which is totally dorky. But he's six feet tall, has an awesome body, and dresses like a rock guitarist—which he is, though of course he and his band haven't been discovered yet. He usually wears tight jeans, black boots, a black T-shirt, and a black leather jacket. He and his band,

Nocturne, play at some local clubs and coffeehouses. They've played a few school dances, too.

"Great," I said shyly.

"Do you want your present now or at dinner tomorrow?"

"Um . . . I guess at dinner." I didn't want to open anything in the school hallway with people looking at me. Dork factor.

"Cool. See you tomorrow, then." He leaned over and kissed my cheek and then disappeared into the crowd of kids spilling into the hallways between classes. Still a little flushed, I went to English class and sat down next to Mina, who was touching up her lip gloss. For my birthday she had already given me a bottle of my favorite perfume—Clinique Happy—in homeroom.

"Vic's taking me to dinner tomorrow," I told her.

"Awesome," she said, putting the cap on her lip gloss and slipping it into her backpack. "You have to get him to find a friend for me so we can go out together. Preferably someone as hot as he is."

"What about the drummer in his band? Don't you think he's cute?"

"Definitely."

"You know . . ." I ventured. "We *could* double

with you and Mark. I mean, you two could go as friends."

"Not until he gets a normal haircut."

I made up my mind to work on that for homecoming, but before Mina and I could talk some more, Mr. Dobbs strode into the room. Of all the teachers at Pacific Cedar, he was the nicest. He rarely gave homework. He was also into music—and not oldies. He was always asking us what we had on our iPods, what we were listening to.

"Okay, everybody, today we're starting a unit on *Dracula*."

I glanced at Mina. *Dracula* sounded more interesting than *Beowulf* or Shakespeare. Or dangling participles and transitive verbs. And definitely more interesting than *A Tale of Two Cities*—my father said when I was older, I'd appreciate it more, but for now it was my least favorite book ever.

"Okay, here's a copy of the book for each of you," he said, passing out paperback books to everyone. "*Dracula* was written by a man named Bram Stoker. The author was born in 1847 in Ireland. He was a sickly boy. In fact, he spent his childhood bedridden until the age of seven. It definitely affected him in more ways than just being sick. It was as if, when he got older, Bram Stoker felt like he had to make up for being a boyhood weakling by becoming an incredibly gifted athlete at Trinity College in Dublin."

Mr. Dobbs, with his blond hair and beard, began pacing up by the blackboard. "And you know, it's a funny coincidence that we're doing *Dracula*, because two of the main characters in the book are Lucy and Mina, and we have a real-life Lucy and Mina in our class." He smiled at the two of us. "Has anyone ever told you two that?"

Mina shook her head. "No. But I think I once saw that in a movie."

"Neat coincidence," Mr. Dobbs said. "Okay, guys, let's open our notebooks and I'll give you a bit more background on this very interesting classic novel."

I opened my spiral notebook and started writing while Mr. Dobbs walked around the room and continued telling us about Bram Stoker and vampires.

"Bram, short for Abraham, was the theatrical critic for Dublin's *Evening Mail*. He did that on the side, while working a civil servant job. In 1878, Henry Irving, a world-famous actor, offered Bram a job as an actor-manager at London's Lyceum Theatre. Bram accepted and moved to London.

"Bram eventually acted as Henry Irving's manager. People said he had a ridiculous devotion to Irving—who could be temperamental, like a lot of creative people. Bram was so devoted to Irving that his wife and son grew to despise the actor. In fact, his son hated Irving so much—and he was named Irving Noel Stoker after his father's friend—that later on he dropped the Irving entirely and just went by Noel Stoker. He snubbed his father's best friend by refusing to use his own first name."

Mr. Dobbs leaned against his desk. "Whether or not Dracula was modeled after Irving is up for discussion, with some scholars saying yes, and some saying Dracula was based on common myths about vampires at the time, including Vlad the Impaler—a particularly brutal and bloodthirsty fellow. My guess is the truth is somewhere in the middle."

Aimee Levinson raised her hand.

"Yes, Aimee?"

"Are we going to get to see a movie about Dracula?"

Mr. Dobbs shook his head. "Sorry, but I want you to concentrate on the book, not the *Cliff's Notes,* and *not* a movie. To make sure there's no cheating as far as that's concerned, the tests are going to be pretty detailed, and we'll be looking at some ways in which the book differs from popular movie versions and from what we all have sort of come to assume is true about Dracula."

"Damn," Mina whispered to me. "No *Cliff's Notes.*"

I smiled. Mina was really smart, but she wanted to move to New York City and study drama at NYU. And anything that didn't have to do with drama class pretty much meant she didn't care about it.

After English class, Mina and I went to our lockers, where we met Mark. He was easy to spot—he was six-foot-four and, as my dad said, "all arms and legs." He had reddish-brown hair, and it looked like Mrs. Carnahan got him but good with the clippers the night before. His hair was about a quarter inch long all around.

Mina hurriedly put her books away and packed her backpack. Mina's mother was picking her up from school that day so she could go get her hair cut—*professionally*. Mina's family was loaded, unlike the Carnahans. Then again, it's easy to have a lot of money when you have only one child. Mina gave me a hug. "Okay, birthday girl, see you tomorrow. Don't let any vampires bite you on the way home." She winked at me.

Mark looked at us like we were nuts.

"We're doing a *Dracula* unit in Mr. Dobbs's class," I offered.

"Lucky. We're doing *Romeo and Juliet*."

"Well, at least you can use *Cliff's Notes*," Mina said. "Later, Mark. Love the haircut." She winked at him, then sighed and took off down the hall. I stuffed my books in my backpack, and Mark and I left school and walked home.

"You coming in?" I asked him when we got to my house.

"Yeah."

"What's that look?"

"What look?"

"You've been smirking since we got out of school." He had. This stupid, lopsided grin. I just assumed it had to do with Mina, but maybe I was reading too much into their teasing lately.

He just shrugged. I took out my huge key ring and unlocked the front door. Stepping inside I smelled something cooking. Which was impossible. My father didn't even know how to turn on the stove. And he didn't let delivery people come to the house—and takeout wasn't an option either.

"Dad?"

"In here," he called from the direction of the kitchen. I wasn't even sure he knew where the kitchen was—that's how little he went in there.

Mark followed me as I walked through the living room to our big kitchen. My mouth dropped open. The table was set, with flowers in a vase, a white linen tablecloth, long tapered candles in silver candlesticks, and our good china—I don't think we'd ever used it before. The china just sat in a cabinet collecting dust. And there stood my dad—in one of my mother's old aprons, no less—stirring a pot.

"Dad? You feeling okay?"

He smiled and came and kissed me on the top of my head. "Happy birthday, Luce."

"How did you . . . get groceries and flowers and stuff?" I was completely stunned.

"My partner in crime." My father winked at Mark.

I turned around. Mark was grinning.

"So that was why you were smirking."

He nodded. Our eyes met for a minute, and I silently mouthed, *Thank you*. This was a big deal for my dad. In fact, Dad actually looked happy.

"It was your dad's idea. He gave me a list and everything, and my mother dropped all this stuff off."

"Wow . . ." I didn't know what to say. I almost felt like crying, I was so happy.

Mark and I sat down at the kitchen table and drank sodas—he likes root beer, and we keep a supply on hand for him. I drink Diet Coke. Mina is a Mountain Dew fan—the more caffeine the better, especially when she has rehearsals five days a week.

Mark and I talked and hung out with my father. Around five thirty my dad served us spaghetti—the thin angel-hair kind—with tomato sauce, garlic bread, salad, and for dessert, an honest-to-God homemade chocolate cake. One side sort of leaned way down to the left, but hey, it was the thought that counted. Dad even lit sixteen candles.

"Make a wish, Lucy," Mark whispered after they sang a very off-key version of "Happy Birthday to You."

My wish . . . I had no idea what to wish for. I was the girl from the house only the Munsters could love. The girl whose father never left the house. The girl with no mother. Where did I even begin to wish? But finally I thought silently, *I wish for my dad to be better. To leave the house. Like when my mother was alive.* Then I blew out the candles—I got them all in one breath, too.

Dad and I and Mark sat around eating cake, talking, laughing—it was so perfect. Then Mark stood to go home around seven thirty.

"Tonight's laundry night. You don't have your laundry in, you ain't wearing clean clothes for the next week."

I stood and gave him a hug. "Thank your mom for me, too."

I walked Mark to the door, and when I came back to help Dad clean the kitchen, he wouldn't let me. "No, no. You go into the living room. I haven't given you your present yet."

"I thought the dinner and the cake were my present."

"Nope. I have something important to give you."

I shrugged and went into the living room. I sat in my favorite chair, a big mushy one that I sank into all comfortably. It always felt like home sitting in that chair. I remember curling up in it with my mother and her reading me *The Velveteen Rabbit* over and over and over again. When I sat in the chair, it was like sitting in her lap somehow. Dad went into his study and came back with a small rectangular wrapped present.

"Before you open this, Lucy, I have something to tell you." He looked very solemn.

"What?"

"The present is actually from your mother."

I stared at the gift on my lap. My father had used enough tape to wrap an elephant. What could be in it?

"Mom?" When I said the word, it sort of felt weird. We never really talked about her. Not very often, at least. "How?"

"Lucy . . . when I met your mother, I was fresh out of the Ph.D. program at UCLA, and an expert in ancient languages and medieval culture. She was this beautiful woman with black hair just like yours, and an amazing story I didn't quite believe until she handed me the gift that's in your lap right now. . . . Open it."

I tore off the paper and looked down in my lap at a book. A leather book.

"It's her diary. And the diary of her mother and grandmother. And great-grandmother. And now you."

"Me?" I ran my hand over the soft black leather cover and then opened it. The first pages were written in a delicate script, and the paper felt stiff—handmade and extra thick. The edges were rough and the script looked like it had been written with a fountain pen.

"Lucy . . . you know your mother's name was Lucy. And so was her mother's. And her mother's mother."

"Family name. You told me that."

"I know. But your great-great-grandmother, also Lucy, in fact, was friends with Bram Stoker."

"Dracula's Bram Stoker?"

He nodded. "She was the inspiration for Lucy."

"She was?" I thought of Mr. Dobbs's class.

"Yes. And that's not all." He took a deep breath. "Lucy . . . that journal in your hands tells of the lineage of women who challenged Dracula. The real Dracula."

"The real Dracula." Okay, now it was official. My father had lost it. Big-time. C-R-A-Z-Y.

"He was real, Lucy. And he was very, *very* dangerous."

"Dad . . . that's insane. It's a novel. You can't tell me you believe in vampires. I mean, yeah, Goth people down in the clubs who want to pretend to be vampires, maybe. But real vampires? Dad . . . come on." Dad was a scholar. He was brilliant. People like that didn't believe in ghosts and vampires and pirates and all that made-up stuff.

"You'll need to read that diary to be convinced. But you're sixteen now, and you need to be prepared. Because Dracula has never stopped in his quest for Lucy and Mina."

"Mina?" I thought of my best gal pal. Coincidence, I told myself uneasily.

"Think, Lucy. Has anything . . . I don't know . . . strange . . . happened lately? Anything that sort of made you feel scared? Cold? Made the hair on the back of your neck stand up?"

I thought of the face at my window the other night when I couldn't sleep, but decided I wasn't going to give my poor crazy father anything more to be nutty about.

"Lucy, Bram Stoker worked for a man named Henry Irving, considered the nineteenth century's greatest living actor. And a vampire. At least according to your great-great-grandmother. She toured America with their acting troupe. They took a train from New Orleans to San Francisco, and your ancestor, Lucy Barrows, was a beautiful young actress with long black hair, porcelain skin, and blue eyes the critics compared to sapphires. Irving couldn't resist her. He was utterly captivated. As much as a vain, egotistical man could be. As much as a vampire could be."

There was that V-word again. My dad believed in vampires?

"Lucy feared for her life," he continued. "And she escaped when they reached San Francisco. Over time she made her way north and established her lineage. She studied everything there was to know about vampires, and she put it in that book there. And now you need to learn everything there is to know. Your life depends on it. Now that you are sixteen, your powers will grow. And so will Dracula's."

"Dracula?"

"He's here. Somewhere in Seattle. Trust me, Luce, if you look around you, it's going to be like a veil has been lifted from your eyes, and you're going to see clearly for the first time in your life. You'll be able to see things others don't, because you'll know the truth, whereas other people will convince themselves they're seeing things."

I looked at him skeptically.

"Think about it, Lucy. If you saw a person vanish into the fog, you'd tell yourself he hadn't even been there in the first place. That you'd imagined it. But if you knew it was possible for a vampire to shape shift and disappear into the fog, then you would really see him. I know it sounds insane. If your mother hadn't gotten sick, she would have been preparing you all this time. But we lost her, so now it's up to me . . . and that book."

I flipped through the pages until I saw what I recognized as my mother's handwriting.

"Um, Dad?"

"Yes, Lucy?"

"This is a little weird."

"I know."

"A lot weird."

"I know."

"I mean, like, crazy, you-need-Prozac weird."

"But it's the truth."

"Is that why you hide in this house?"

"Oh, Luce . . . that and just missing your mom. After she died, even breathing hurt without her."

My eyes welled up. I wondered if someone would ever love me that much. "I think I want to go read some of this book now," I whispered. In fact, I just wanted to be alone.

"I understand."

I stood up, feeling sad. Dinner had been so perfect, and now this. He had finally lost it. "Thanks for dinner," I said softly. "It was really special." I thought of adding, *Until you decided there really is such a thing as vampires*. But I kept my mouth shut.

I took the book and kissed my father good night. Then I went upstairs to my bedroom and sat down in my beanbag chair.

Mina.
Henry Irving.
Bram Stoker.
Vampires.
And me.

Suddenly my already slightly weird life had gotten decidedly weirder. I opened the book and something fluttered to the floor. I reached down and picked up a photo. It was facedown. I turned it over.

"I don't believe it," I whispered.

Looking up at me in the sepia tones of a very old picture was me. Well, not me exactly, but someone who looked just like me. Her hair was pulled up into a loose bun, and she wore what looked like a velvet dress with a sweetheart neckline. She was dressed in old-fashioned clothes, and she was very elegant, but she looked like my twin. She had high cheekbones and eyes that turned up ever so slightly at the outer corners. I was staring at me from another time. The original Lucy, my ancestor.

Chapter 4

May 3, 1885

Dearest Diary,

    I am sitting here by lamplight, doors locked, terrified. Ever since the ship to America, I have felt the eyes of Henry Irving upon me, upon my every move and every breath. He even fills my mind when I sleep, invading my very dreams.

    The crossing was horribly rough, the seas high, and I stayed in my cabin, but even that did not shield me from him. I swear upon my life that I could hear him in my mind, calling me to him. He is not an easy man to please. He's quickly made cross, angry. As an actress, even when I heard I had the role, I envisioned Mr. Irving dismissing me from the company. When Mr. Stoker said I would be allowed to come to America with the troupe, I was delighted. But now I fear I may pay for this trip with my life. I cannot sleep, and every night I toss and turn, unable to put my mind at ease, to rest. I hear him calling to me in my sleep. Isn't that odd? And, diary, I have seen a face at my window. A face with red eyes. I know not who he is, yet he terrifies me. I feel he knows me in ways that are improper.

We took the train from New Orleans—oh, that city is strange and has its own secrets, I fear. In three days' time, we will arrive in San Francisco. I have sworn to myself that I will slip away in the night. I will escape both Stoker, with his uneasy closeness, his worrisome personality, and Irving, with his angry tirades. I will escape them even if I am penniless. I swear it.

And one more thing, dear diary. I scarce dare write this. But I believe Mr. Irving has made some sort of devil's pact. I don't know why. But he is fearful of daylight and always lurks in the shadows. In the realm of Lucifer. I swear it. I feel it. God save me. God help me.

Signed,
Lucy

Chapter 5

Christmas Day, 1919

Dear Diary,

It doesn't seem like Christmas. No tree, no peppermints or oranges. No Christmas carols. My mother has passed, one year ago to this day, bless her soul, and now it is up to me to carry on this mantle of responsibility—no holidays for me.

I felt the evil one's presence yesterday when I went to town to market. I dared not turn around. Mother said never to engage him openly, never to look him in the eyes—he has too much power. I had to abandon the idea of even the most modest of Christmas suppers and quickly come back to my house. I thank God for the dogs that protect me so fiercely.

I never rest. I tire easily. At night I sleep only behind locked doors, two dogs at the door, one across my bed. I now realize I must impart my mother's wisdom in this book. Whosoever shall take

37

this mantle from me after I die must know you cannot kill a vampire with an ordinary pistol. You cannot hang him or even drown him, binding him in chains and throwing him into the briny seas. No, you must burn him as he rests in his coffin or drive a stake through his heart. You must be fearless. Fearless!

Oh, how I wish more than anything that this responsibility weren't mine to bear, but my life and the evil one's are inextricably bound.

I must sign off now. May God watch over me this night.

Signed,
Lucy

Chapter 6

O kay. So I was from a long line of crazy
women. I wanted to just dismiss the whole insane idea of vampires, the way I dismissed my father's eccentricities. But I had a couple of problems.
One, there was that face at my window that night
when I couldn't sleep. And more than that, some
very unusual coincidences were cropping up.

My best friend's name was Mina.

My English teacher, Mr. Dobbs, was starting an
entire unit on Bram Stoker.

My sometime boyfriend, Vic . . . his last name
was Irving, same as the guy my great-great-
grandmother was afraid of.

And my father had, now that I thought about it,
seemed to have spent his entire life consumed with
monsters and Latin manuscripts. If his story of my
mother was correct, he was just a language professor
until she dragged him into all this. And though my
memories of my mother were faded at best, she certainly never *seemed* crazy to me.

I decided to read her portion of the diary. But what I found wasn't a diary at all. No . . . by the time she wrote in the book, she was writing to *me*. To her daughter.

> *My darling daughter Lucy,*
>
> *I've told Dad to give you this book for your sixteenth birthday. I know I won't be there, but if you are holding this, then I am there in spirit.*
>
> *And I suppose right now you think I am crazy. And that your dad is crazy. But we're not. You know, there were actually times when I was your age that I wished Grandma were crazy. It would be so much easier to just explain all the strange happenings away. More than that, then I wouldn't have had to deal with vampires. But right about my sixteenth birthday, I started having dreams.*
>
> *And my guess is you have them, too. A face at the window; a very deep, powerful voice calling to you. Intense eyes glowing kind of red. Scary. And the dreams will get worse, Lucy, until you learn to control them—which this book will show you how to do. Dreams of Dracula, fog, stormy sea crossings, and hiss-*

ing, screaming vampires. They were part of my teen years—I know, like it isn't enough to just worry about raging hormones and homework.

All parents want is to raise their children in safety and security. We want to create a perfect world, a beautiful place of butterflies and rainbows. But the world isn't always like that. There's war and poverty and drugs and murder. And now that you know our family's secret, the world will become a bit darker, Lucy. You'll start to see shadows and fog and feel a cold presence. It is him. Dracula. The most powerful vampire who ever walked this earth.

Each woman in our family has given birth to a daughter to carry on the legacy of fighting Dracula. And he, I assure you, has a son in our town who is your destined enemy. It's how it has been since before you were born, and how it has been since before I was born.

Oh . . . and one more thing. The evil one is so powerful, he can walk in daylight, darling. Just as in Bram Stoker's book—you see, it's Hollywood that has created some myths. But yes, he can wander in daylight, so you need to be careful all the time. Though he clings to darkness, don't think sunrise makes you safe.

Enough for one night, one birthday. I love you so much, sweetie. I know you're confused, and I wish I were there to help you. But for now know your father is there. And you are more powerful than you could ever realize. Believe that. Believe in you.

And happy birthday, my darling Lucy.

Love,

Mom

I sat there, shaking. I had to believe. The dreams. The cold feeling. I know it sounds like I was going crazy, too, but in my heart, something told me that this was all real. That vampires were real.

That Dracula existed.

In Seattle.

As if high school weren't bad enough.

Chapter 7

I was being burned alive. Screaming, I slapped at the flames as they licked my arms, scorching me. I could feel the heat on my face. I looked around. Vampire bats flew in every direction. I tried to cover my face. I ran from my room and then the house, but the bats followed me. I could feel their furry bodies against my face, their leathery wings flapping against me. I screamed over and over again. Shrieking, trying to fling them away from me.

And finally, thank God, I woke up. I was having a nightmare.

I felt out of breath, and I was all sweaty and hot. I looked at the floor. I had kicked my comforter there in a heap. I flicked on my light and looked up, half expecting a bat to be hanging from the ceiling, but there wasn't one. Instead it was just my normal room, the walls covered in posters of Paris and New York City and Venice and Switzerland. I had never been to any of those places—not with my father afraid to leave the house. But I dreamed of going someday. I wanted to travel the world.

Sleep was going to be impossible now. I didn't want to fall back asleep and pick up my dream where it left off. No, thanks. I climbed out of bed and decided to go down to my father's study and look at all his books. I mean, I couldn't read Latin, but I thought I could at least check out the pictures and see if they shed any clues as to my mother's strange legacy.

I pulled on my blue terry-cloth bathrobe—our house was always drafty—and crept downstairs, trying to avoid the spots on the steps that creaked really loud. I had on my thick sweat socks—I always wore them. Seattle's damp, rainy climate meant the floors were always cold. I padded into my father's study and turned on the green banker's lamp on his desk.

Walking over to his tall bookcases, I ran my finger along the spines of the ancient books he collected. He must have had forty different copies of *Dracula*. I had never noticed before. I pulled one out. It was quite dusty and looked like it was from Stoker's time. I opened it and noticed handwriting in the margins. It looked like a woman's writing, delicate and graceful. Certain sentences were underlined, and then with an arrow the writer had pointed to the margin, where she wrote, *Untrue*, or *Yes, this is so*. I put the book back on the shelf and went over to my dad's desk. Old manuscripts with drawings of strange creatures were scattered. I sat down and began looking at them all. There were gargoyles and vampires, men with dark capes, and creatures with horrifying features—long nails and bloody teeth, sunken eyes.

"Lucy?"

I screamed and jumped. "Dad . . . God, you scared me."

"Sorry. What are you doing up? It's three o'clock in the morning, honey."

"Dad, you gave me a diary that says I have to fight some ancient vampire who's been after me and my mother and my grandmother and great-grandmother. . . . I mean, was I *supposed* to sleep after that?"

He smiled and looked a little embarrassed. "No, I guess not."

"If it wasn't Mom's handwriting, I wouldn't believe it. I still don't know what I believe. Dad . . . you know, all I've ever wanted is to be normal. Is that so much to ask?"

He sat down in a big wing chair by his desk. "No, it's not. What I wouldn't give to go back in time to when she was here. Even with this legacy, she had a way of making the world seem right. Did I ever tell you about when she and I met?"

I shook my head.

He leaned his head back. "When I met your mother, I fell instantly in love. I was a bookworm—um, you'd say I was a dork. And I couldn't believe this wonderful, vibrant woman was in love with me. She blew into my life like a hurricane. She loved rock music—I grew up with your grandparents, who listened only to Perry Como."

"Who?"

"Don't ask. Anyway, she loved rock and concerts, and she liked pizza with everything on it but the anchovies. She loved the rain. She liked to go out in it and just get drenched. I never met anyone quite like her. When she told me she needed my help interpreting old manuscripts, I didn't believe what I read. She had ancient texts on vampires—how to kill them, how they appear. In Africa, for instance, there's a belief that they kill livestock. Some say they can shape-shift—turn into wolves and bats. Some say you can kill them with spikes through the heart, with fire, with silver bullets. But to me, when I first met her, I was interpreting old myth. To her, they were real."

"But . . . real vampires, Dad?"

"If I hadn't seen one with my own eyes, I don't know if I would have believed it."

"You saw one?" I asked skeptically.

He nodded. "We were in Prague tracking down an ancient manuscript. We were out in the country-side, at a small church. Holy ground, or so we thought. We were so naive then. We were behind locked doors in a library hidden in the basement of this two hundred-year-old monastery. And he mate-rialized right in front of our eyes. There was an el-derly priest helping us. He believed in all this myth. His grandmother, he told us, had passed along sto-ries of a vampire who would steal young virgins and kill them in the woods outside their village. I dis-missed talk like that as the rantings of an old man. Then a fog came into the room from nowhere. It seeped under the door, and then there he was. The vampire."

"What did he look like?"

"He was very, very tall. At least six-foot-two. And he had long, dark hair, and his muscles—in his neck, his face, were very sinewy. His eyes were black. And he was pale. I could see his fangs. He drew his head back and then he bit the priest. Right there. On the neck. Drained him. Dead."

"What? Dad . . . in front of you? Oh, my God. I would have freaked."

He nodded. "I was too stunned to move. But your mother grabbed a crucifix made of wrought iron that was flanking the doorway to the library. She used it like a spear and made a move to pierce the vampire's heart."

"My mother? The woman who used to cut my peanut butter sandwiches into heart shapes? The one who made me a mermaid costume in kindergarten, complete with tiny seashells she sewed onto the neckline?"

He laughed. "Yes, Lucy. The heart-shaped-peanut-butter-sandwich maker was unbelievable. She was incredible. A warrior. And this vampire was scared of her. Well, maybe *scared* isn't the right word, but he definitely didn't want to do battle with her. He commanded the fog all around him—speaking in Latin—and disappeared. So did the priest's body."

"What did you do after that?"

"We hightailed it back home—to you."

"How old was I?"

"A little baby. We had left you home with Nana Marie. We thought you'd be safer. And after that, we started thinking maybe it would be best if we were more careful. We stopped traveling. We doubled our efforts to figure out how to kill Dracula and to understand your mother's lineage. And we started to realize that we were drawing him to us. He was obsessed with your mother, so even as she established her lineage here, he brought some of his lineage to Seattle, determined to make her his bride."

"Well, he picked a great place, didn't he? It rains all the time, the sun never shines, and there's enough fog here for a whole army of vampires."

"Well, your great-great-grandmother didn't think all that through when she migrated to the Pacific Northwest. She would have been better off in the middle of a hot, arid, sunny desert."

"So did you and Mom ever discover what kills them?"

"Stake through the heart. Beheading."

"Gross."

Dad nodded. "But the good news is that your godfather was a huge help in bringing vampire slaying into the twenty-first century."

"Uncle Jack?"

Dad nodded. Uncle Jack was at *least* as weird as Dad. No, weirder. A famous physicist, he had an IQ my father said was so high people came to study him like he was a science experiment himself. However, like some of the great geniuses throughout history, Uncle Jack could barely function in the real world. For example, he refused to wear socks because he hated matching them after they went through the wash—especially since he sent all his wash out to the dry cleaners, which could get pretty expensive. He just couldn't fathom how to use the washing machine—or the coffeemaker, toaster oven, dishwasher, or the TV remote.

"Uncle Jack came up with this," Dad said as he opened a metal file cabinet with a key and brought out a wooden box, which he unlocked with another key. Inside was nestled a bottle of clear liquid.

"What's that?"

"Drop this into a vampire's drink, and it'll kill him."

"What's in it?"

"Liquid garlic. At a concentration so high it's fatal to a vampire. It would give you and me a major stomachache. And here." He opened another drawer and pulled out a bottle of perfume. "This will really get him."

"Perfume? You're going to try to kill a vampire with perfume?" Yup, Dad had lost it once and for all.

"It isn't ordinary perfume. In fact, it's not perfume at all. Garlic . . . you know what its compounds are?"

"Um, no, Dad. I really never thought about garlic. Except on garlic bread at Mario's Pizzeria."

"Well." Dad looked excited. He was always excited when he got to talk about anything scholarly. "Garlic actually has sulfur compounds in it."

I tried to look interested, but frankly, discussing garlic in the middle of the night was a big yawnfest.

"Sulfur," Dad continued my mini science lesson, "is colorless. And it can sometimes be odorless. And you can find sulfur in volcanic ash, in cinnabar, and even in Epsom salts."

"Fascinating," I said, without much enthusiasm.

"Ah, but you should be interested, Luce, because this perfume isn't really perfume at all. It's got high concentrations of sulfur and allicin, and even has a touch of volcanic ash to it, along with scallion juice, all masked with high doses of gardenia."

"Uh-huh."

"Well, you can wear it to ward off a vampire getting too close. Better yet, if you find yourself in a fight with a vampire, you spray it in his eyes. Voilà! It's like vampire pepper spray."

All right, now I'd heard everything. "Vampire repellent? This is what you and Uncle Jack came up with?"

"Exactly. You take it," Dad said to me. "And start wearing it to school. Then keep the bottle in your purse."

I took the bottle in my hand and sprayed a tiny bit on the inside of my wrist. It smelled okay. A little heavy, kind of like when there's too many flowers in a funeral home or a hospital room, or too much incense in a church or something, but it wasn't horrible. Still, I didn't think I'd suddenly take to wearing eau de vampire.

"Promise me you'll wear it."

"Sure, Dad."

"No, Luce, a real promise. Look me in the eye."

I hate when he does that, because I just can't lie to him. Like the time Mina and I sneaked out of her house and went to a party and drank too much. I told him the truth. Mina? She lied. But my dad was all I had.

"Okay, I promise," I said.

"Cross your heart."

"Am I twelve here, Dad?"

"Cross your heart," he said in this silly sort of voice, like he was being all bossy.

"Fine," I said and rolled my eyes while making an X sign on my chest. I took the perfume and the garlic serum.

"And remember, beheading also works. So does a stake through the heart, but you have to be sure you get him. Wooden stakes? No good. I mean, maybe back in the Middle Ages, but trust me, they're not strong enough. You'd need one made of a very strong metal—steel, for instance. And you'd have to be very strong yourself to get it through his heart, which is why Uncle Jack and I turned to modern chemistry."

My father and Uncle Jack were the two smartest men I knew. I had to hope that if vampires were real, and if they were after me, that whatever they'd concocted would work—modern chemistry or not. Because I knew one thing: There was no way I could ever behead a vampire. I mean, I couldn't even stand dissecting the frog in eighth-grade science class.

Chapter 8

"What happened to you?" I asked Mina on Friday at our lockers. She looked awful.

"I am *so* over this place," Mina snapped.

Of course, Mina is always saying that. She hates Pacific Cedar, hates the Goth kids who sometimes stare her down—she's just too rich and too perky for them—hates the whole downtown-Seattle scene. Hates coffee and rainy days.

"So what else is new?" I shrugged, kind of ignoring her. We've been best friends since we got assigned to work on a science project together a couple of years ago. Come to think of it, she was my lab partner for frog dissection, and she couldn't cut the frog up either.

"No, this time I'm totally over it. Last night a wolf was in my backyard, howling at the friggin' moon. I swear, that may be fine for *National Geographic* and the Discovery Channel, but I can't wait to move to New York City and get the hell out of

Seattle. You won't see a wolf baying at the Empire State Building."

I froze. "A wolf?" Suddenly I had no spit. I mean, my mouth was totally dry.

"Yes, a wolf."

Mina's father is president of a company that makes something having to do with computers. All I know is that they live in a mansion made of stone and cedar that backs up onto a land preserve with tons of trees and woods, with a water view in front of them. Mina's an only child, and they're so rich they have a "staff"—not just a housekeeper, like my dad and I used to have. But "staff," as in chef, maid, butler, and gardener. But despite their living near the woods, I don't think I'd ever heard anything about a wolf in her backyard.

"Are you sure it wasn't a dog? It could have been a husky or something."

"Look at me, Lucy Hellenberg."

I turned to face her, and she slammed her locker shut.

"Do I look stupid to you? Hmm? Do I? Of course it wasn't a dog. I know what a dog looks like. Bow-wow, 'come here, Rover.' No, this was a big, huge wolf with sharp teeth, and a howl that made my mother freak out, take a Valium, and go to bed. It decided to pace outside my window for half the night. My father even called the police to send Animal Control over."

"I didn't think you were stupid, Mina. It's just . . . Never mind." I tried not to let her see the worry I felt.

"Oh . . ." she shook her head. "I'm sorry. I know I'm being b-word. I just didn't sleep at all last night. The wolf was creepy."

"It's okay."

The two of us started walking toward class when Mark came and found us. The Three Musketeers. He looked as tired and messed-up as Mina. And it wasn't just his classic Mrs. Carnahan ax job on his hair.

"And what's with you?" Mina snapped.

"Don't ask."

"Can't top my night," she said as we pushed and maneuvered our way through the crowded hallway.

"Oh, it might. Apparently I was sleepwalking last night."

"What?" I grabbed his arm. I mean, I've known him since we could take baths together. He never did *that* before. "Sleepwalking?"

He nodded and ran his hand through what little hair he had. "My mom says maybe I'm worried about taking my driver's test. Yeah, right. I won't ever be able to actually drive the family car, so why the hell would I worry? I feel like a weirdo. Sleepwalking." He shook his head from side to side. "And I was having really weird dreams, too."

Mina made a sort of crooked smile. "Hmm . . . I had a wolf in my backyard. But I wasn't so *freaky* as to sleepwalk. You win."

"Win what?"

"Your story beats mine. You are weirder."

"Well, we'd have to take a vote on that. I mean, there is your phobia of butterflies. Like the gentlest, prettiest things on earth and you're freaked out by them. Wait a minute . . . a wolf?" He looked completely confused.

"One story at a time," I said. "Did you wake up?" I asked Mark.

"Kind of. I was halfway out the back door when my father found me. He brought me back inside and then kind of shook me awake."

"I thought you weren't supposed to wake up sleepwalkers," Mina offered.

"Yeah, well, my father was afraid I'd wander off and, I don't know, get hit by a car or something."

"Poor baby." Mina gave him a hug and patted his cheek, which made Mark turn red.

"What was your dream about?" I asked.

"I bet I know." Mina smirked. "I bet it was about that new girl in Ruthless's class. The blonde."

"No," he snapped. "I don't like her, Mina, so shut the hell up already."

She held up her hands. "Touchy . . . my God. Take a deep breath, there, Marky-Mark."

The bell rang—meaning we had better get into homeroom fast or we'd have to report to the office for late passes. We started scrambling.

During homeroom, I couldn't concentrate. The weird vampire factor had just multiplied. Mina sat next to me in homeroom—Mark's homeroom was in the classroom across the hall. I reached into my backpack and pulled out the perfume vial my dad gave me. I gave myself a squirt. I'd have to ask my dad if Uncle Jack could make a guy-smelling one for Mark. I couldn't imagine Mark would agree to walk around smelling like flowers, and with the weird things happening, I was worried about my two best friends. Then I reached over and squirted Mina.

"Hey!"

"New perfume," I said, shrugging.

"Ew! I don't like it," she hissed at me. "Luce, you wear what you want. I like Calvin Klein."

"Sure," I said, then put my perfume away.

Mrs. Mahoney shouted, "Settle down!" She started taking attendance. I sat there listening to kids say, "Here," as she called their names. She said, "Paul Holt." He said, "Here," and then out of the blue he turned around and stared me down.

"What?" I snapped.

Paul had bottle-black hair the color of coal, and he spiked it straight up and applied gel with electric-blue coloring to the tips. He wore a dog collar around his neck. He would have been scary except he wasn't very big—he was so skinny I thought even I could knock him over.

"What's with that stink?"

"It's perfume," I said, squinting my eyes to look tough—at least a little bit.

"Well, it's disgusting. Don't wear it anymore."

"Shut up." Like I was going to listen to some Goth vampire wannabe. Or . . . nah. I put the thought from my mind.

Mrs. Mahoney gave me a dirty look and continued taking attendance. I zoned out and started thinking about Mina and Mark. I decided I was the unluckiest girl in Seattle. No one could be having the problems I was having. I mean, vampires made other girls' problems, like zits, water weight gain, and even hopelessly strict parents seem like nothing at all. I made up my mind that no matter how insane I sounded, I would have to tell Mark and Mina about the vampires. Even as I thought that, I shook my head. I hoped they believed me—though I wasn't sure I believed it all yet myself. But I had to admit life at Pacific Cedar was getting stranger by the minute.

After all, even the evil Mrs. Ruthless couldn't compare to Dracula.

Chapter 9

After school, I begged Mina and Mark to come to my house. Mina didn't have rehearsal—the Drama Club was apparently working on scenery, and she doesn't do manual labor. Vic had told me his older brother was going to drive us to dinner at a place called Serendipity near the water. It was supposed to be a very hot place to eat. His brother was then going to go to a club—and we'd text-message him when we wanted him to pick us up. I had a few hours until eight, when they were coming to get me.

After pulling out my janitor-size key ring and unlocking all the locks, saying hi to my dad, and grabbing a bunch of junk food, I went up to my room with Mina and Mark and shut the door.

I went to my dresser, where I had hidden my mother's diary in my underwear drawer, and took out my mother's book. Then I told them, as best I could, about my mother, the diary, and my sixteenth birthday. I even told them about the night I was sure I saw a face at the window.

"Okay," Mina said, "you know, I think your dad is a real sweetie pie, even if he's a little bit odd and has no fashion sense. But, Luce . . . vampires?"

"Do you believe me?" I asked Mark.

Mark was quiet for a minute. "I've lived two doors down from you forever, Luce. I knew your mom." He gave Mina a little bit of a dirty look. "And I've *seen* your dad's manuscripts. I'll admit it sounds a little . . . um . . . freaky. But I don't know. Maybe it's true."

I opened the book and showed them passages from the 1800s, all the way to my mom.

"This one is from my grandmother," I told them.

A week ago a black wolf came to the yard. He attacked my beloved dog, King, and nearly tore away the flesh at King's neck. I was terrified at the wolf's fierceness. King was valiant, though. He fought the wolf, protecting me, as I was standing on the back porch. Eventually the wolf limped away, whimpering a bit.

I wrapped King's neck in bandages, and applied poultices. I thought I would lose him, and I stayed with him night and day, but he survived. His voice, however, did not. Poor

King cannot bark. He cannot make a sound. His vocal cords must have been damaged. And now it is completely obvious to me. Without his loud bark, King cannot warn me when the evil one is near. This was the wolf's plan all along.

I looked at Mina. "What color was the wolf in your backyard?"

"Black," she whispered.

"Shit," Mark said. "Man, oh, man, we're dead. We're vampire bait."

Mina nodded. "Vampire appetizers."

"Well," I said quietly, trying to sound calm, "it may not be as bad as all that. First of all, now we know, right? So we can be ready."

"Ready?" Mina half shrieked. "Ready? I mean, what are we supposed to do? Kill them with wooden stakes through the heart?"

"Actually," I said, "my father says that won't work. Unless we were a whole lot stronger than we are—and there's always the chance the stake could break. Which is why we have this." I pulled out my perfume and I tried to make my voice sound positive, when deep down I wasn't so positive at all.

"Ugh . . . is that what you squirted on me in homeroom?"

I nodded, and squirted her again, and then squirted Mark.

"Ugh!" he said as he smelled the perfume. "I have enough problems getting dates without smelling like a girl. Jeez, Lucy . . ."

"Look, I promise to ask my uncle to make one that's more guy-smelling. More masculine."

"What's in it?" Mina asked, sniffing her wrist.

"I'm not sure. Concentrated sulfur and . . . I don't know. Crap that repels vampires. Volcanic ash. I don't know. When my father gets excited I kind of zone out. He was babbling about sulfur and compounds last night. My godfather designed it."

"What is he? A perfume guy?"

"No. A chemistry professor with the world's seventh-highest recorded IQ."

"Why do I not find that surprising?" Mina asked. "Only you, Luce. Well, it's worth a shot, I guess," Mina said. "This perfume is no Calvin, but . . . well, I don't feel like being wolf bait."

Mina took the diary and started looking at the entries. "Oh, my God, I am totally freaked out. Read this one." She held out the book to Mark and me.

Darling Lucy,

Beware of anyone with the last name Irving. I used to think that the vampires would change their family name, wouldn't flaunt the connection to Henry Irving. I mean, that makes sense, doesn't it? But I was wrong. I think the ego of Dracula prevents him from changing his name. They live openly. There are signs, if you look for them. Though they can go out in the day, they act hungover, tired, irritable if it's a sunny day. They prefer the shroud of fog.

They are conniving. They are cunning. They are clever. They will go after your friends. It's best to be alone, darling. Your father and I had one loyal friend, Professor Van Helsing, and, well . . . he's now the family cat, turned into an animal by the dark powers of Dracula. So be careful, Lucy. And know wherever you are, whatever you do, you are like me and the women before me. You are far stronger than you realize, Lucy. As you'll read, you can train to challenge him, train to protect yourself.

I love you.

Mom

Mina looked at me and said one name: "Vic."

"Can't be," I whispered.

"Can't be?" Mark sputtered. "Your mom couldn't have been more specific. You have to break up with him."

Vic. The guy I'd liked since I was thirteen years old and he literally ran into me in the hallway and nearly broke my nose. We flirted with each other for two years before he finally asked me to go to the movies. We'd see each other at parties. We hung out together sometimes. He never dated anyone else. I never dated anyone else. But we weren't quite girlfriend and boyfriend. I don't know what we were, other than that I still really, really, really liked him.

"Look, guys, I'll be careful."

"You'd better spray so much of this perfume on that he can barely breathe—vampire or not," Mina said.

"Great," I muttered. "This is ridiculous. Vic would never hurt me."

"He did almost break your nose once," Mark offered.

"Yeah," I shot back, "you often hear about vampires killing people by smashing into their noses."

"Well . . . it could be." he shrugged.

My head hurt from thinking about all this. "And

look, I don't know if we all should hang out together anymore. At least, not until I learn more."

"Why?" Mina asked. "Because of what your mother wrote?"

I nodded.

"Look, babe." Mina stood and hugged me. "We've been friends through crushes, Mrs. Ruthless's class, detention. . . ."

"My grandfather dying," Mark said, "my bad haircuts, the time I had to have my appendix taken out, the summer that my father made me mow lawns to pay for a new couch after I accidentally spilled grape Kool-Aid on it . . ."

"My mother's ridiculous rule about dressing for dinner, the time I dyed my hair blond and it turned orange . . ." Mina was smiling.

"Okay, you guys win." I grinned. "If it was the other way around, no way would I not be there for either of you."

"Exactly," Mina said.

"Okay, so we've got to stick together. And we've got to be careful. And we need to figure out a way to get rid of this Dracula guy once and for all. That way I can get on with my life and live in peace. My dad, too."

"Deal," Mark said.

"Deal," Mina said.

"Deal," I said. Then for good measure I squirted us all with vampire perfume again. We were really starting to smell so sweet that it was making *me* gag.

I could only imagine what Vic would think.

"And what's the deal with your cat?" Mina asked.

"I don't know. I'm getting to the point where I believe in vampires. I think. But my cat?" I stood and crossed the room, opening the door. "Professor V?" I called out. "Here, kitty."

"Meow," was the reply. Professor V, big and midnight black and fat, padded silently down the hallway and came and rubbed up against my leg and purred. I scooped him up and brought him into my bedroom and laid him down on the bed and started scratching behind his ears.

"You guys," I asked, "what's the average life expectancy of a cat?"

Mark shrugged. "About fifteen years, if you're lucky, why?"

"Well, according to my dad, Professor V came along the first year my parents were married, which would make him"—I calculated in my head—"nineteen. Don't you think that's kind of old for a cat?"

"He doesn't act old, do you, boy?" Mina said, tickling him under his neck. "Besides, I've heard of cats that old."

"Okay, Professor, if you used to be a person, meow twice," I said, looking my cat square into his yellow eyes. He didn't meow.

"I'm just losing it." I sighed and flopped back on my bed.

"Losing it or not," Mark warned, "no hickeys from Vic . . . and maybe you should wear a turtleneck."

"Yeah, and maybe I should also wear a giant crucifix."

"Good thinking," Mark said. "And for dinner, order something with a lot of garlic in it."

"Bad breath, smelly perfume, giant crucifix, turtleneck . . . anything else I can do to seem like a dork?"

"No, that should about cover it."

I rolled my eyes. I'd only had the biggest crush on Vic from the minute I first saw him, and now my friends and I were trying to think up ways to make sure he never wanted to have anything to do with me again.

Chapter 10

Vic's brother drove an amazingly cool black Mustang. They pulled into our driveway right at eight o'clock, and Vic came to the door, very politely, and rang the doorbell.

"Dad," I called out, "I'm leaving."

"Okay," he shouted back from the study.

My father had never asked me Vic's last name—and I prayed tonight wouldn't be the time he decided to. Dad came out of his study and smiled this big, goofy grin.

"What?" I asked him.

"You're wearing your perfume. And you look beautiful, by the way."

"Thanks." I had decided to wear black jeans, an Abercrombie sweater, and high-heeled black boots. My hair was curly and loose, past my shoulders—but not Chia Pet explosion levels. A good-hair day. "And it would be great if Uncle Jack could make some cologne-type vampire repellent for Mark. He had a sleepwalking incident—and Mina saw a wolf."

"What? Wait a minute, Lucy Victoria Hellenberg, you didn't tell me this. You can't go out now." My father cut in front of me and blocked the front door.

"Dad . . . I have a date—with Vic. Please don't embarrass me."

"You're not taking this seriously enough, Lucy."

I looked at him, pleading, "Dad, please let me go on my birthday date with Vic, and I promise starting tomorrow I will take this seriously. First thing in the morning, I swear. Look." I took my perfume spray out of my purse and squirted myself. "Happy?" I wanted to kick myself for mentioning the cologne for Mark, but I was worried about my friends.

The doorbell rang again. I was panicking. Dad looked at me, but finally he nodded.

"Okay. I suppose I can't expect you to give up your whole life. But be careful."

He stepped aside, and I undid all the locks. Vic stood there with a single red rose. "Hey, Luce."

"Hi, Vic. This is my dad."

"Hello, Mr. Hellenberg," he said to my dad, and stuck out his hand.

"Hello," Dad replied and shook Vic's hand. "Come on in."

"Um, Dad . . . his brother's driving us. I don't want him to have to wait." *And I don't want you asking Vic all kinds of questions.*

"Oh . . ." Dad looked disappointed. "Okay, well, you two have fun. Be home by eleven."

"Dad . . . uh, it's my birthday dinner."

"Oh. Right. Of course. Then midnight. And call me if you, um, need me. You have your cell phone, right?"

I nodded.

"Okay, kids, have a good time."

How Brady Bunch *dorky, Dad.*

Vic and I left and walked down our creaky front steps. He handed me the rose and held open the car door for me. Vic's brother, Jude, sat in the driver's seat and gave my father a wave. Jude was dressed in black from head to toe, and had a bunch of piercings and spiked hair. I waved to my dad too, but I could see that his eyes were open wide. He didn't look happy. In fact, he looked completely upset.

I tried not to worry about my father. Vic held my hand, and as always I could barely think of anything else.

Jude drove, focusing on the road as Vic took his

index finger and traced shapes on my palm. My heart was pounding—his touch was so sexy. After a few minutes Jude started coughing. So did Vic.

"You guys okay?" I asked.

"Yeah . . . I think it's your perfume," Vic said. "Maybe I'm allergic."

"Well, if you're allergic, I am, too," Jude said. "It's giving me a killer headache."

"I'm sorry."

"Don't worry about it," Vic said. "It smells beautiful. And you look great."

I smiled. Maybe my perfume was a little heavy. And maybe the Irving boys were vampires. Vic leaned over and started nuzzling my neck. I jumped.

"What?" He looked at me.

"Nothing. Just tickled."

Jude pulled up in front of the restaurant. "Okay, guys. I'm going to be at the Underground. Text me."

We climbed out of the car. As Jude pulled away, I wondered what to think of Vic and his brother. Vic brushed a stray strand of hair from my face. "Hey, whatcha thinking, Lucy?"

"Oh, nothing."

"Come on, let's go inside."

We entered the restaurant. It was elegant, with a fountain as we walked in, and thick velvet curtains on the walls. Enya piped in over the speakers. The place was very romantic, and Vic slipped his arm around my waist. The hostess seated us at a table at a window overlooking the water, which we really couldn't see in the darkness outside.

"Jude kind of scares people," Vic offered. "His whole Goth look. Hope you don't get in trouble with your dad or anything."

"Dad . . . he worries a lot. But he trusts me."

"You're lucky. What does your dad do again?"

"He used to be a college professor. Now he works on books."

"What kind of books?"

The hair on the back of my head stood up, and my arms prickled. Why was he suddenly interested in what my dad did after two years?

"Oh, you know, books. I don't really know."

The menu was expensive. Usually the only time I ate out was when Mina's family invited me. Mark was always more broke than I was, and Dad never left the house. Mina's mother, however, felt, according to Mina, that eating out was a hobby, like some people played golf or did crossword puzzles. Mina's mom ate out and went shopping. Mina's parents were always very nice to me, including me like I was their own daughter. Mrs. Crane even bought me clothes when she took Mina and me shopping. I think they felt a little sorry for me. But I could only imagine how upset they would be if they found out that I was single-handedly responsible for a wolf showing up in their backyard.

Vic reached across the table and took my hand. "Want your birthday present now?"

"Sure," I said. He had never gotten me a gift before. Last Valentine's Day he gave me roses and a card. But never a present. Not a real present.

He had hung his leather jacket over the back of his chair, and with his free hand he reached into its pocket and pulled out a small, wrapped gift, which he slid across the table.

I took my hand from his and slowly unwrapped the present, trying not to feel nervous, and hoping no one was looking at me. When I got the box unwrapped, inside was a black velvet box. I lifted its lid, and nestled on the velvet was a gold locket that glittered in the candlelight.

"It's beautiful," I whispered.

"It's antique. You like it?"

"I . . . love it." I had never owned anything like it before. It was heart-shaped, and the gold was shiny, but because it was old it had etchings on the front that made it look special, different. The chain was fairly strong but intricate. I opened the locket. Inside were two old pictures, black-and-white, a man and a woman.

"Who are they?" I whispered, my throat dry.

"I don't know." He laughed. "Isn't that funny? My grandfather said he found it in an antique store. He said it's bad luck to change the old picture out. Could be two people in love, he said. But read the back of the locket."

I turned it over in my hand.

To Lucy, from your admirer

"That's so sweet."

"Yeah, but it was on the locket already. That's why my grandfather said you had to have it. It would be perfect for me to give to you. And doesn't she look like you?"

I nodded, feeling dizzy. I put it around my neck and then took a big gulp of water. The photo of the woman was the same picture from the diary. Black hair pulled up in a loose bun, enigmatic smile. It was Lucy. I fingered the gold chain. Who was the handsome man whose picture faced hers? And why did Vic's grandfather have the locket? A little too coincidental for him to have simply found it in an antique shop. I tried not to worry. Our waiter came and we ordered dinner—I got pasta. He got steak, which he ordered very, very rare.

"A little bloody," he said to the waiter.

Okay, aside from the fact that really rare meat makes me queasy, I felt like I was lining up two columns. In column A, I had "reasons Vic is an evil, bloodsucking vampire." In column B, I had "reasons Vic is the same, hot, sexy, sort-of boyfriend he's always been." Bloody steak? That went over in column A, along with coughing and choking around garlic perfume. In column B I had a beautiful locket, a red rose, and the firm handshake he gave my father. Okay, maybe the locket belonged in both columns.

We finished dinner, and we decided to walk around downtown for a little while. It was chilly, and Vic slipped an arm around my shoulder. He coughed again.

"My perfume?" I looked at him.

"Yeah, weird, isn't it?"

I nodded. The moon was out. I half expected him to turn into a wolf, but instead Vic pointed to a star. "Make a wish, Lucy."

I had just one.

Star light, star bright, first star I see tonight, I

wish I may, I wish I might, have this wish I wish tonight.

I wish . . . that my boyfriend isn't really a vampire.

Was that so much to ask?

Chapter 11

Dear Diary,

    I decided that if all my ancestors—and my mom—wrote in this book, I'd better write in here, too.

    I'm Lucy Hellenberg. Sixteen. Not too fat or too thin. Pretty, but not perfect. I have Chia Pet hair— black—and a few freckles on my nose, pale white skin—easy to have in rainy Seattle. My eyes are blue- gray. I look like my mom. That's what my dad says. I think I do, too.

    I remember only bits and pieces of my mother. It's like trying to remember something that's on the tip of your tongue. I have little memories of her, like I remember one time when I was maybe four. It was a rare sunny day. Mom used to say every day was a gift, but sunny days were extra special and you had to treat them like that. We went out into the backyard with a goose down comforter and spread it out on the lawn, then sank into it. Then we lay on our backs and stared up at the sky and looked for

79

shapes in the clouds. I thought every cloud looked like a bunny. I remember my cheek was next to hers, and it was just a perfect day. I didn't know then that she was sick or that she was going to die. If I had, I couldn't have picked out or planned a more perfect memory of her.

Now I wonder about all my memories. They're tinged now with the idea that the whole time my mother was loving me and raising me, she was protecting me from a line of vampires. And now I have to wonder if Vic is somehow related to them.

Our date last night started out okay. Except for the fact that he and his brother sneezed around me with my new eau de vampire stuff on. Don't ask!

Dinner was expensive, sexy, and delicious. He gave me a locket for my birthday—which is a whole long story, but it was still very sweet of him. We talked about school a little, but then more about his music and what we want to do after high school. I've always been that girl who never knew what she wanted to be when she grew up. Mina . . . she wants to be an actress. Mark wants to be a meteorologist. Just kidding. That's our little inside joke. He says he wants the easiest job in the world—a weatherman for Seattle. All he has to do is say, "And tomorrow, *cloudy and overcast with a seventy percent chance of rain." Vic wants to be a musician.*

Anyway, after dinner we text messaged Jude, and when he came to get us, he had this totally scary guy in the car. His name was Seth, and he was dressed in black from head to toe—okay, so that's not so scary, because plenty of Goths go to our high school. But he had maybe thirty piercings—he had five piercings in one cheek alone—and he was wearing dark sunglasses. The really black Ray•Bans kind where you can't see the person's eyes behind them at all. And he was really, really irritated by my perfume. Not only that, he was asking me a ton of questions—where was I from, where my parents were from. Like, who asks about parents when you just meet somebody? Vic held me closer in the backseat. We were kissing and stuff. But the vibe . . . this guy Seth seemed like a serial killer, I swear. He even talked in this sort of creepy voice. And I couldn't tell how old he was. Like, he wasn't our age, and he didn't seem to be twenty-one or twenty-two, like Jude. But he wasn't old either. Just creepy.

When we got to my house, Vic walked me to the door. He kissed me good night—a really hot kiss. And I was embarrassed, because I knew I was going to have to unlock all the locks and just look like this freaky girl who lives in the Munsters' house with her paranoid father. So I took out my keys, but then Dad surprised me totally by opening the door. And then, out of nowhere, Professor V leaped from on top of the tall wooden cabinet in our front hallway onto Vic's head. It was like I was seeing it in slow motion. Vic screamed, and Professor V clawed his face. I was screaming at Professor V, and Dad was trying to pry our cat off of Vic's head. Nice date. This could only happen to me, right? I mean, if there was a "bad ending to a date" contest, who could top that? Mina once puked all over a date—she ate bad shrimp and got food poisoning—so that's kind of in the running. However, pet cat suddenly acting like a wild tiger and clawing boyfriend's face? Well, need I say more?

Then Jude and Seth jumped out of the car. They both came running. Vic was bleeding, and I swear, I swear, cross my heart, that I saw Seth grow fangs. I know that sounds nuts. Beyond nuts. But he did. His canine teeth grew really pointy.

Then, as suddenly as he went crazy, Professor V jumped into my arms and started purring like a kitten. He nuzzled under my chin and meowed softly. I felt so bad for Vic, but I was convinced I'd just seen my first vampire. I offered to let Vic come in and wash his cuts, but he said no, not to worry about it. Seth, meanwhile, had his arm around Vic's shoulder and was like, "Come on, dude, let's get you home."

The three of them left the porch, and Dad and I and Professor V went inside. I held my cat up, nose-to-nose with me.

"You did that on purpose, didn't you?" I asked him.

Then I looked at Dad. He was white as a ghost. Said he could tell they were all vampires—all three of them. Then he said, "Lucy . . . something funny's going on here. What's Vic's last name?"

I was so busted.

And so, dear diary, not only did my cat claw my boyfriend's face, and not only did that pretty much ruin our good-night kiss, but I am grounded.

Dad says it's for life.

Ugh.

I hate being a teenager.

Chapter 12

How ws yr date

IM grounded

U r

Yup

Sucks

Yup

I text-messaged back and forth with Mina the next morning. Then she called me after her facial, and I filled her in.

"Fangs?"

"Yeah. Fangs. Big ones. Pointy ones. Suck-your-blood ones."

"You know, I've heard of people getting fake

84

fangs made so they can pretend to be vampires. It's like this vampire subculture. I Googled it."

"Poser vampires?"

"Yeah."

"Well, trust me, this guy was way too into blood for him to be a poser. He was practically drooling over Vic's cuts."

"So now what?"

"Now what? I want my old life back—as pathetic as that sounds. I want to go back to just being the girl with the weird dad in the Munsters' house. *Not* the girl with a vampire problem. So the sooner I accomplish that, the better. I'm going after these guys."

"Do you have a plan?"

"No, I don't have a plan. But that's never stopped me before. Remember that time I stood up to the science teacher about the cruelty of dissection? I had no plan then, either, but it ended up before the school board by the time I was through. And now students can elect not to dissect."

"Well, I sort of have a plan."

"What?"

"Mr. Dobbs. He's a Dracula expert all of a sudden, right? Well, I had this hunch. And guess what?

He's related to Bram Stoker—I mean, going back a while, but yeah."

"How do you know?"

"Google, Lucy." Mina was, like, a major Internet addict. It was how she did half her shopping. And she had this eBay account and bid on designer purses, which she collected the way Mark collected baseball hats. Only she spent a *lot* more money on her collection.

"Well, Mr. Dobbs's being related to Bram Stoker could be bad. I mean, after all, my ancestors hated Bram Stoker."

"Could be. But I sort of get this good vibe from him. I mean, how bad could he be if he never gives homework and has a stash of Hershey's Kisses that he doles out after tests? So what do you say we feel him out about the whole vampire thing? Maybe he'll have some suggestions."

"Okay. Can't hurt."

Well, it could, but what the hell?

Vic called me that afternoon.

"How's your face?" I asked him.

"Okay. Man, your cat does not like me."

"He's never done anything like that before. I'm really, really sorry."

"It wasn't your fault. Did you have a good time?"

"Yes. Right up until the attack of the killer cat."

"Um . . . Luce?"

"Hmm?"

"Is everything okay? You're acting just a tiny bit weird. I mean, am I crowding you?"

Crowding me. No, I've been waiting a year for this relationship to get more serious, only now I think you're one of the friggin' undead.

"No-o-o," I said slowly. "You're not crowding me."

"Okay. So we're cool?"

"Yeah."

"Great. Listen . . . so you want to go to homecoming together?"

"I'm grounded right now."

"Why?"

"Long story." God, I liked him so much. I mean, maybe his brother and Seth were vampires, but Vic was the same old Vic. At least, I hoped he was. So I heard myself say, "Never mind . . . Sure . . . sure. I'll be able to talk my dad into it. Let's go to homecoming."

After I hung up, I wondered what the hell was wrong with me. This same old Vic liked raw meat. We weren't talking *Romeo and Juliet*. We were talking undead and living. Can't get more star-crossed than that.

∗

Mina, Mark, and I all, separately, spent the rest of the weekend Googling everything we could find out about Bram Stoker, Dracula, Vlad the Impaler, Henry Irving, killing vampires, and even Goth trends. We learned about fake fangs, filing your own teeth down into fangs, and vampire legends. We learned about vampires that supposedly sucked the life out of babies. We each read stories of people buried alive in the Dark Ages, before modern medicine made the pronouncement of death scientifically official, awakening in their coffins and screaming bloody murder, only to be dug up again and discovered to be alive—hence rumors of vampires. People were so afraid of being buried alive, they sometimes tied a string to the corpse's finger, and had that lead through a hole in the coffin up to a bell on top of the grave—so just in case you were buried alive you could alert the grave diggers. The thought gave me the creeps. We learned about silver bullets, garlic, mirrors, bats, bug-eating half-dead zombies, and rituals. In short, we tried to become vampire experts in as short a time as possible. My eyes were blurry from staring at my laptop all weekend.

Mina called me Sunday night. "Do you realize if I studied this hard for school, I might actually be an A student?"

"Yeah, and if shopping were a subject, you'd be given a full scholarship for college."

"Find anything that would help us figure out a plan?"

"Nope. But at least I now know that some vampires in Africa supposedly suck cow's blood. I'm a regular vampire trivia whiz."

"Ah, but did you know that you can actually buy a vampire field guide to slaying the undead? There are a lot of people out there who believe in vampires."

"Yeah, but I bet none of them have Dracula after them."

"Well, let's hope Mr. Dobbs can help us."

And so, without any real plan, Monday after school Mina and I stayed and asked Mr. Dobbs if he could give us some extra help on *Dracula*.

"Sure thing, girls." He leaned against his desk expectantly. We were alone in his classroom. "Well? What are you having trouble with?"

"First off, I was wondering if you believe in actual vampires," I said.

"And that has to do with *Dracula* how?"

"Um, just curious."

"Just curious, huh?"

I nodded expectantly. "Well, do you?" With that, I pulled out my vampire repellent and squirted him.

"What the heck is that?"

"Perfume."

"Okay, girls, what's up? Spraying your English teacher with perfume? Don't you think that's a little bit . . . inappropriate?"

"But do you like how it *smells*?" Mina asked, squinting her eyes and trying to look tough.

"And do you believe in *vampires*?" I asked.

Mr. Dobbs walked over to the door and poked his head out in the hallway. The crowds of Pacific Cedar students had all gone home except for the kids stuck in detention in the lunchroom.

He turned around to face us and walked quickly until he was about two feet away. "How did you find out I'm related to Bram?"

Mina's eyes widened.

"Are you going to bite us?" I asked, holding out my spray bottle.

"Bite you?" Suddenly he started laughing hysterically.

"What's so funny?" Mina snapped. "Because if you are, we're calling nine-one-one."

He laughed even harder. "I'd love to hear that call."

"Stop laughing!" she snapped.

"I can't help it."

Well, we *were* accusing our English teacher of being a vampire.

Mr. Dobbs continued laughing and shaking his head.

"All right, girls, have a seat."

Mina and I each sat down, but I kept my vampire repellent in my hand. I wasn't taking any chances.

"Why don't you start by telling me why you believe in vampires?" he asked.

"Why don't *you* start by telling *us* how it is you've kept hidden the fact that you're related to Bram Stoker?" Mina said. I think because she's been a little spoiled her whole life, she can be pretty bossy sometimes when she talks to people. Even teachers.

"And do you think vampires are real?" I needed to know. Maybe I needed someone outside of an old book and my dad to tell me whether or not vampires existed. Even seeing Seth's fangs with my own eyes didn't 100 percent convince me.

"Fine. To answer you, Lucy, I *do* believe in vampires. Though if either of you tells anyone else, I'll deny it, of course."

"Are *you* a vampire?" I asked.

"Would I tell you if I were?"

"Probably not."

"Well, I'm not, so you can both relax. I'm one of the good guys."

"How do we know?" Mina asked, again squinting her eyes at him.

"You're just going to have to trust me. The whole reason we're even doing a *Dracula* unit, when the rest of the school is doing *Romeo and Juliet*, is that I wanted to tip you off to who I am and how I can help you. I knew you were both smart enough to figure it out."

I felt a little bit relieved. "You can help us?"

He nodded. "You're not alone."

"Okay, if that's true, then what's your story?" Mina asked.

"Hold on." Mr. Dobbs went over to the classroom door again, but this time he shut it. Then he spoke quietly, almost in a whisper. "I am related to Bram Stoker. He was my great-great-uncle."

"Cool," said Mina.

He nodded. "When I was a kid I was totally into the idea that the man who wrote *Dracula* was related to me. But my parents never wanted to talk about it. Apparently there was a lot of feuding within the family over his estate and over his legacy. But I was a pretty persistent kid. Eventually they did tell me about some of the rumors—including that Henry Irving was a real vampire."

"Was he?" I asked. "Is he the real Dracula?"

"Well, I didn't know what to think at first. And when my parents finally filled me in on the family legends, I was about sixteen. I was into horror movies . . . and I had quite an imagination. I was convinced there was a vampire in every dark corner, you know?"

"So what did you find out?" Mina asked.

"Well, I became an amateur vampire expert. And I became absolutely convinced that Dracula had followed the real inspiration for Lucy here to Seattle."

"But in the book, isn't Dracula obsessed with Mina?" Mina asked.

"Yeah, and don't be so sure you're not in danger, too. But I think he was afraid of Lucy's power. Lucy is like his kryptonite, you know?"

"I wish I felt powerful," I moaned.

"You're stronger than you think," he said.

"That's what my mother's journal says."

"You have a journal from your mother?"

I nodded. "And her mother before her . . . all the way back to the original Lucy."

"I'd love to take a look sometime. See, as near as I can figure it, something about the young actress Lucy Barrows bugged Irving. He became a bit obsessed. What he didn't count on was her not succumbing to his charms. That was what he was used to—women falling at his feet."

"In the journal, she really doesn't like him or trust him."

"Exactly. And worse, she ran away." Mr. Dobbs laughed and kind of shook his head. "Dracula just didn't count on her being so feisty—and then raising her daughter that way. She was a feminist before her time."

"So you really think Dracula is real?" Mina asked.

"Yeah. I've seen things I couldn't explain. Like a couple of years ago, I went to confront your boyfriend's father over Jude's acting up in class. And Mr. Irving literally levitated in front of me and threatened me. Said I should get out of town if I knew what was good for me."

"Levitated?" Mina asked. "So why didn't you—"

"What? Tell someone?"

Mina and I exchanged glances. Yeah. Right.

"Exactly," Mr. Dobbs said. "Tell someone and lose my job? No one would believe me. Worse, they'd think I was crazy."

"So Jude and Vic . . . are they vampires?"

"I don't know yet. But even if they're not, they're being trained to be. They could be weak vampires, and with their father and grandfather's tutelage, they could become more powerful."

I thought of the time, three weeks ago, when I had a head cold and Vic left me a box of cough drops on my desk. Or the time he burned me a CD of all the songs that meant something to us. Now, what vampire does that?

But of course, there were the things in the other column.

"Well, I know Vic isn't. Or I hope he isn't. He can't be. And I don't think Jude is either. Yet. But Jude has a friend, Seth—and I'm pretty sure he is."

"He's on my chart."

"Chart?" Mina asked.

"Yup." Mr. Dobbs looked pretty pleased with himself. He walked over to the blackboard, above which hung a bunch of maps and things, along with the screen where he projected the occasional movie.

He pulled on a particular map of Central Europe. Then he peeled at some tape and the map of Europe fell away. In its place hung a flowchart. My mouth dropped open. In thick black letters, I read:

> ## Seattle Area
> ## Vampire
> ## Organizational Chart

"Organizational chart?" I asked.

"Think of it as a family tree."

With that, Mr. Dobbs grabbed a wooden pointer and began showing Mina and me all about the vampires in my hometown. In Pacific Cedar Grove. In my high school.

"You don't have Paul Holt on there," I said, thinking of the guy in homeroom who freaked over my perfume.

"He's a wannabe. But his friends—Ronnie, Jake, and Colleen? They're major vampires—their lineage goes back to this guy here." He pointed to a vampire name, Count Bogdonavich.

"Who's he?" I asked.

"Just one evil, evil vampire. A Russian."

"So how is it all these vampires come here to Pacific Cedar, to Seattle?" Mina asked.

"Climate. Commerce."

"Commerce?"

"You'd be surprised how many of them go into software development. They can work nights, sleep days, never leave their tech nests except to hunt and feed."

"So they don't need coffee to stay up all night, just a little blood. Now I've really heard everything," I said, rolling my eyes.

"But the main reason they come here is him." He pointed to a name. "Count Dracula. Henry Irving."

"You're saying he's still alive?" I raised an eyebrow.

"Yes. His family buried an impoverished actor who bore a strong resemblance to Irving, made up by the Lyceum Theatre's makeup artist to look exactly like Henry Irving. After the poor actor had been drained of much of his blood, of course. And Henry Irving is the great-great-grandfather of Vic."

And there on the flowchart, circled in red, was

the word *Vic*. The one guy I'd liked all through high school. With a question mark next to his name.

Vic.

The guy I was going to the homecoming dance with. I needed a dress—preferably a little black velvet number—new shoes . . . I needed to get my hair done. Maybe I'd get it blown out straight. And to top it all off, I needed a lovely corsage of garlic to go with my ensemble.

Chapter 13

After school, Mina's mother picked us both up. Her mother was obsessed with her looks. There was nothing that woman wouldn't do for her appearance—Botox, Brazilian wax job, breast implants, and enough makeup to fill an entire department store counter. Inevitably she had advice for Mina and me every time she saw us. I needed to accentuate the arch in my browbone more—she had a woman who did eyebrow waxing who was "the best," according to Mrs. Crane (who insisted I call her Bebe). Mina, according to Bebe, needed a nose job. Mina had a perfect nose, but Bebe felt there was nothing that couldn't be "a little more perfect."

"You can give Luce a ride home, right, Mom?" Mina asked as we piled into the back of the BMW convertible she drove—in sky blue to match Bebe's eyes.

"Sure, Mina, honey. You know, girls, we could stop off at the Wild Mane Salon and get a little brow touch-up, maybe pick up some shampoo and conditioner. I love that lavender shampoo they use. It's right on the way."

"No, thanks, Mom." Mina leaned into me and whispered, "Unless they make garlic shampoo."

"What was that?" Bebe asked, her auburn hair blowing in the breeze with the top down. She looked like she was thirty years old—a lot of times people thought she and Mina were sisters.

"Nothing."

My house wasn't far from school, so we were there in a few minutes with traffic lights. I was still absorbing Mr. Dobbs's "organizational chart" in my mind. The sheer number of suspected vampires in my hometown was staggering.

Bebe pulled up to Chez Munsters, the tires of her car crunching on the gravel. "Who's that?" she asked, seeing someone sitting on my front porch steps.

"Holy crap," Mina said.

"Mina!"

"Sorry, Mom."

I groaned as I climbed out of the car. "Could my life get any worse? Please tell me. Anyone?"

"Well, who is it?" Bebe asked again.

"Ms. Harris," I muttered. "The school shrink. Thanks for the ride, Bebe."

"Call me," Mina said. "As soon as she leaves."

I rolled my eyes and walked toward my front porch. Ms. Harris was sitting on the top step patiently.

"Hi, Lucy." She smiled. "This was on my way home, and I thought I'd drop by. Your father appears to be home, but he's not answering the door. I knocked a few times and rang the bell."

"Yeah, well, he likes his privacy," I said. "He's not very . . . social."

"I was hoping to talk to you both, actually. Principal Becker was concerned. He says you were supposed to let him know how you were doing, but you haven't."

I shrugged. What was I supposed to say?

Ms. Harris was a thin woman with pale blond hair she wore in a precision bob. She had pretty skin, with naturally rosy cheeks, and light eyes behind silver-framed glasses. She looked around my dad's age. She wore gray slacks and a pretty soft gray sweater with beading around the neckline. It was a chilly afternoon—typical Seattle, with overcast skies and a rainy chill to the air, so she had on a pair of fuzzy pink wool gloves and a fuzzy pink scarf.

"Sit down by me, Lucy," she said, and patted the step next to her.

There was no escaping her, so I sat down.

"Lucy, when things are tough in your life, who do you turn to? Who do you go to when you have problems at school, for instance, like the little incident in Mrs. Ruthen's class?"

"Well," I said, "Mina is my best girlfriend, and Mark is my best guy friend. I've known him since we were both babies."

She nodded and looked intently at me. "Is that it?"

"Well, I can go to my dad. I know he's different, but we're really close."

"I'm glad, Lucy, but you know, it's not fair for you to have to be on your own in so many ways. I hear you do all the grocery shopping, have all the responsibilities of an adult. You need time to be an ordinary teen."

I felt like laughing hysterically. Sure. And who was going to let the vampires know?

"I'm still an ordinary teen, I think. Besides, who's to say what's ordinary?"

She looked at me quizzically. "Well, I suppose that's a good point. Do you think maybe I could come in for a few minutes?"

I couldn't imagine my father agreeing. Then, to

my total shock, I heard the sound of lock after lock being unbolted, and the door opened a tiny bit.

"Lucy?" My father said from the crack in the door.

"Hi, Dad."

"Who's this, Luce?"

She stood up. "Carolyn Harris, Pacific Cedar High's school psychologist. We've spoken on the telephone before."

"David Hellenberg." He stuck out his hand and smiled at her, even opening the door more and venturing a step or two onto the porch.

"I've read some of your work, Professor."

"You have?"

"I double-majored in English as an undergrad. I read one of your journal articles on the intricacies of translating Homer's *Iliad*."

"Would you like to come in?"

"I'd love to," she said, smiling.

"I'll make us all a pot of tea."

My father? A pot of tea? I looked at him as he opened the door wide for Ms. Harris. His hair was combed. His shirt was tucked in. He wasn't wearing his moth-eaten gray sweater.

He led the way through the front hallway,

through the living room—which was neat as a pin, no newspapers and magazines scattered all over the coffee table—into the dining room.

"Sit down, Ms. Harris."

"Please, Professor Hellenberg, call me Carolyn."

"Fine, if you'll call me David."

She blushed.

Okay, so this was beyond freaky.

Ms. Harris sat down at the dining room table, and I followed Dad into the kitchen. He had a tea tray set up with a china pot—I didn't even know we had one—filled with hot tea, a plate with sugar cookies, and a sugar bowl and teacups.

"Dad? What's with all this?"

"Oh, nothing," he said, smiling. "This tea set used to belong to your grandmother. Pretty, isn't it?" He held out a teacup, which was painted with delicate roses.

"I don't mean the tea set. Dad?" God, he could be so professorish sometimes. "Do you *like* Ms. Harris?"

"Like her? No. I mean . . . ," he stammered, "um, I mean, she seems like a very fine person. We've spoken on the telephone a couple of times."

"You have?"

He nodded.

I tried to decide which was weirder—vampires or my dad with a crush. It was a tie.

He carried the tea tray in to Ms. Harris—Carolyn—and served us all tea. He was positively charming—funny and smiling, and telling her stories about traveling in Prague and Moscow and the countryside of England before my mother had died. He even regaled her with a funny story about translating dirty limericks from old English.

For her part, Ms. Harris seemed completely fascinated by my father. She hung on his every word and laughed at all of his bad jokes. She even patted his hand once. Then, after talking about how she felt I needed a little more support, and it would be a bit healthier if my dad could be more involved in my school and my life, it was like they forgot all about me and started talking about everything from traveling to Shakespeare.

I was bored out of my mind.

"Can I go up to my room, now, Dad?"

"Huh? Oh, sure, honey."

I stood to leave and Ms. Harris smiled at me. "Oh, Lucy, I heard you and Vic Irving are going to the homecoming dance together."

Dad's eyes opened wide. "Really?" Then, when her head was turned toward me, he gave me a *Lucy Victoria Hellenberg, you are in so much trouble* look.

"Yes." She smiled. "Vic is such a nice young man. A good student. I'm on the decorating committee for the dance. Vic is on the fund-raising committee—they're having a car wash Saturday to raise money, you know. Anyway, he mentioned it."

My father didn't look too happy with me.

"Oh . . . I'm sorry," Ms. Harris said. "Did I say something I wasn't supposed to, Lucy?"

"That's okay." I smiled as best I could. I was so dead. If the vampires didn't get to me, Dad would. Busted. So busted!

"If you're worried, David," she said, "you should come and be on the chaperone committee."

I could not imagine *anything* more humiliating than your parent being a chaperone for a school dance. I was so grateful that was one thing I didn't have to worry about. My father? Leave the house and go to a crowded gym to chaperone a bunch of obnoxious kids—let alone a vampire or two?

And then my father uttered one word. "Sure."

My life was going from bad to worse to total social disaster.

Chapter 14

Your father said what?!"

"You heard me," I snapped into the phone. "He said sure. As in yes."

"Ugh. So much for majorly hooking up on homecoming night."

"No kidding."

"Which is just as well, you brat."

"What?"

"Vic? You're going with Vic? I mean, you saw Seth grow fangs, you read your mother's book, you saw Mr. Dobbs's chart. Wait," she squealed. "There was an article on this exact problem in *Cosmo Girl*."

"An article on vampire boyfriends?"

"Not exactly, but close."

I rolled my eyes and waited while I could hear her through the phone rifling magazine pages. She bought every single magazine at the grocery store every week and month. We would lie on her big king-size bed and flip through them whenever we had a sleepover at her house. She came back on the line.

"Here it is! 'Is Your Relationship Toxic?' It's a quiz to see if your boyfriend is bad for you or not."

"You're going to compare having a boyfriend who may—or may not—be a vampire, with a toxic relationship? He can't help it if his family is made up of vampires. And it doesn't mean he is. That's like saying if your father is an alcoholic you have to become one."

"Well, here's the first question. Yes or no. 'Do your friends avoid spending time with you and your boyfriend?'"

"Um, no. I mean, until recently, you had every intention of going to homecoming with me and Vic."

"That was before I decided I don't want to become one of the undead. You know, a vampire can just turn you into something like that guy in Dracula who eats bugs."

"You have a major spider phobia, along with your weird butterfly phobia. I don't care what a vampire did to you; there's no chance you'd become a bug eater."

"Okay . . . there's this question. 'Do you avoid telling family and friends that you're spending time with your boyfriend because you're afraid of what they might say?'"

"Oh, you mean they might ask you dumb quiz questions?"

"Come on, Luce. It's a toxic relationship. You shouldn't go to homecoming with him."

"Well, I am. So are you going to go to the mall with me to help me pick out a dress?"

"Well, duh. Of course I am."

"Can Bebe take us tonight?"

"Sure."

"Don't you have to ask her?"

"Give me a break. This is *Bebe* we're talking about. If she doesn't visit Bloomingdale's once every forty-eight hours, she breaks out in hives."

✳

True to form, Bebe took us to the mall. She's actually kind of fun to shop with, because she gets in these moods where she just wants to spend money. I remember one whirlwind trip when she whipped out her credit card and bought fourteen—count 'em, fourteen—pairs of shoes at Neiman Marcus. She was like a woman possessed. The day-after-Thanksgiving holiday sales? She's a demon shopper.

That night, however, Bebe was depressed.

"What's wrong, Mom?" Mina asked as we pulled into a parking spot at the mall.

She sighed.

"What?" Mina asked again.

"All right, you might as well know. I got the invitation to my twenty-year college reunion. I just want to throw up. I feel old." She pulled down her visor to look in the little mirror. "I look old."

"Mom, that's ridiculous. You look our age, for God's sake. Get over yourself."

"I need a makeover."

"A makeover?" I asked. "Bebe, you're gorgeous. How could they possibly fix you?"

"Well, a little collagen, a little Botox. And I'm getting all new makeup tonight. Youthful. Come on, girls."

We followed her into the mall and left her at the makeup counter. The salesgirl must have felt like she hit the jackpot, because Bebe sat in one of the tall makeup counter stools and said, "I want one of everything. And fast."

"We're going to find Lucy a dress, okay, Mom?"

"Sure." Bebe waved her hand, her long, manicured nails polished to perfection. "Meet you near the food court in two hours."

Mina and I left the makeup counter and went into the main part of the mall. As we walked Mina started rubbing her arms.

"What's up?"

"I'm cold."

"Want my jacket?" I had on a flannel-lined jean jacket, with a black turtleneck.

"Yeah." Mina had on two sweaters already.

"Maybe you're coming down with something."

"I don't know."

We walked some more and spotted a really adorable dress in the window of a shop. We walked over to it, and Mina rubbed her right temple.

"What?" I asked her.

"I wish I knew. I just feel like I'm coming down with something."

I looked at the dress in the window, and from the reflection in the store glass I could see two guys behind us. I squinted. They looked awfully familiar. I grabbed Mina's hand and pulled her into the store. I forced her to duck behind a rack of clothes with me.

"What?" she snapped.

I peered over the top of the clothes rack—a very nice selection of cashmere, I might add.

"I knew it," I whispered.

"Knew what?"

"Over there." I jerked my head.

Standing out in the mall area were Jude and Seth. And Seth, for one, seemed entirely too interested in my best friend, Mina.

"Crap . . . ," I muttered. "*Cosmo Girl* doesn't have a quiz to handle this situation."

Sure. I could just imagine. "Toxic Boyfriends and Their Vampire Families: How to Tell When Enough Is Enough."

Chapter 15

Lucy?" Mina gripped my arm. Her fingers were icy.

"Are you okay?" I looked at her. She was so pale—if Bebe saw her she'd drag her off to the makeup counter for an emergency intervention of blush.

"No." She started breathing really hard. "I feel like I'm going to throw up."

"Let's call Bebe on her cell."

"Wait a minute. I need to sit down."

I looked around the store, but it was wall-to-wall racks of clothes—no place to sit. I glanced outside the store, where Seth stood with Jude. They were hanging out by two benches near a small snack bar.

Mina looked like she was in a trance. She was pale, and her eyes didn't look like they were focusing. She started walking toward the entrance. Toward Seth and Jude.

"Mina? What's going on? Come here," I hissed at her. "Mina!"

She didn't even look at me.

"Damn!" I looked at Mina, and then I looked at Seth. He was staring at her so hard, like he was staring *into* her. Something was definitely wrong.

I reached into my purse and pulled out my cell phone and dialed my father.

"Dad?"

"Yeah, Luce?"

"Um . . . now, don't panic."

"What's wrong?" I could hear the panic in his voice. *So much for "Don't panic."*

"Dad . . . we're at the mall, and Seth—that guy from the other night—and Jude, Vic's brother . . . they're here and . . . Mina is getting sick. She looks pale, and I just don't have a good feeling about this. She's like, not listening to me even though I'm talking to her. Hold on." I went and grabbed Mina by the arm and physically turned her away from the entrance and back into the store. "She's wandering, Dad. And it's like the lights are on but nobody's home."

"Oh, no . . ."

"What?"

"Don't panic, but you need to get her out of there."

"Why? What is it?" Now it was my turn to freak out.

"He's mesmerizing her."

"Huh?"

"Henry Irving was known as a mesmerist. It was part of his worldwide renown. Kind of like a hypnotist. He did it as a parlor trick, you know, something to entertain people with. But underneath that parlor trick was something a lot more sinister. It was a method to hide his vampirism."

"So they're hypnotizing her?" I looked over at Mina. She seemed worse. Her eyes were glazed over; her mouth was open. She looked totally out of it.

"Sort of. As the Irving lineage has gotten stronger, as Dracula got stronger, he developed an ability to enter people's minds. To enter their thoughts. Mind control. Mina must be very susceptible."

"How come?"

"She's not afraid."

I looked out at Jude and Seth loitering, waiting for us. I sure as hell was afraid.

"What do you mean? Why does that matter, Dad?"

"Well, you can't be so afraid that you're paralyzed by your fears. But you must have a healthy respect for them, a fear that keeps you on your guard. Mina must have doubts about whether vampires really exist. She doesn't have the protection you have.

She didn't guard against them, because a big part of her probably believes this is all a fairy tale. A myth or a legend. Not real."

Mina started walking away from me, out of the store.

"Crap, Dad, she's heading toward them. She looks like a robot. What do I do?" I went and grabbed her again. "Stay here!" I snapped at her, but I might as well have been talking to one of the cashmere sweaters—because Mina didn't register that she heard me at all.

"Douse her in the perfume, and get her to look at you, connect with you, not him. And then both of you get out of there. Where's Mina's mother?"

"Makeup counter."

"Get to her. And be careful."

I snapped my cell phone closed and took out my perfume and sprayed her from head to toe. She started to gag and retch. A saleslady looked at us.

"Is your friend all right?" I'm sure the lady thought Mina was on drugs.

"Um, yeah. She's feeling a little sick."

"Let me know if I can help you."

Mina continued to clutch her stomach and make quiet gagging sounds.

"Mina!" I took her by both shoulders and tried to get her to look me in the eyes.

"What are you doing to me?" she asked accusingly.

"Spraying you with vampire repellent."

"Get away from me." Her speech was slurred, like she was drunk. "God, that smells. Bad. I like Calvin Klein. You know that."

I put the perfume back in my purse and then grabbed Mina by the shoulders again.

"Focus!"

"What? I don't feel well."

"Mina." I shook her. "Mina . . . okay. We need to go find Bebe and get you home."

"I feel sick; let me lie down." She started to lie down right on the store floor. I glanced over at the saleswoman. She looked ready to call security.

"Get up, Mina. Get up!"

"What's your problem?" she whined.

"My problem is you're being mind-controlled."

"Mind-controlled?" she sneered at me.

"Let's go!" I snapped at her. "You'll thank me later."

I pulled her up and took her by the arm and marched out into the mall. We were in a public place,

I reasoned. They couldn't do something to us out in front of witnesses. Could they?

I ignored them as Mina and I walked toward Bloomies, where we'd left Bebe. I could feel them following us, but I didn't turn around. Eventually they caught up to us by the food court, and Jude tapped me on the shoulder.

"Hey, Lucy, don't you recognize me? Vic's brother."

I wheeled around. "Sure." I glared at him. "I recognize you for who you are," I said.

He gave me a sneering smile. "I bet you do. And aren't you going to introduce us to your gorgeous girlfriend here?"

"No." I grabbed her hand again and started to move.

Seth held out an arm, blocking our path.

"Come on, ladies . . . why don't we grab a *bite* to eat?"

Mina looked dazed again. God, every time she got near this Seth guy, she wigged out on me.

"Why don't you get lost?" I said to Seth.

He opened his mouth, sort of seductively, and licked his lips. I could glimpse his fangs, but Mina seemed oblivious.

"Because I don't want to get lost. I think your friend is really beautiful."

Mina smiled, but it was a robotic smile. Her eyes were glazed over, and it was like nothing was really registering with her. I didn't know what to do. Suddenly, moving people aside and parting the crowded mall like Moses parting the Red Sea, Bebe came, teetering on her designer eight-hundred-dollar shoes.

"Girls! Girls . . . there was the most incredible sale going on." She had an enormous shopping bag in each hand and gestured at her purchases with her chin. "Just *look* at all the stuff I got. I bought stuff for both of you, too."

Bebe prattled on and on, as was Bebe's way. Finally, she caught her breath enough to say, "Mina! You look pale. Are you sick or do you just need some blush?"

"She's sick," I piped up. "We need to get her home, Bebe."

"Well, come on, girls. Good thing I'm a speed shopper. I was going to grab a cappuccino. I'm glad I got here early." Bebe gave a withering look to Seth and Jude and moved us along. Mina was breaking out in a sweat, and I was so relieved Bebe had come when she did. I looked back and the two creeps were just standing there. Then Seth looked right at me. I could hear him—in my mind.

You can't win. I have all the time in the world, Lucy. I have eternity.

Chapter 16

Bebe zoomed us through Seattle in her sports car. The farther we got from the mall, the better Mina looked.

"You girls really shouldn't hang out with guys like that. They're lowlifes. I really *hate* that whole Goth look. I mean, do you like that in a guy? Lucy? Mina?"

"No," I said. "They're just two jerks I know—they're older than us. I date the dark-haired guy's brother."

"Well, Mina . . . I do not want you hanging around with that type. Take it from me, girls . . . go for the geeky guys. They'll make a billion dollars someday building a company, and you'll never have to work a day in your life."

Mina rolled her eyes. She was convinced that she never wanted to get married. And even if she did, she didn't want to live like Bebe. Mina wanted to be an actress and make her own fortune. The two of us were in the backseat, and she leaned over close to me.

"Was I actually flirting with that guy?" she whispered.

"Not exactly."

Mina shook her head. "It's like I remember the last hour but I don't. Like I was in a fog or something. Confused. Tired. And I'm exhausted. More tired than I've ever been my whole life."

"We're going to have to be more careful."

"Did you find a dress, Lucy?" Bebe asked over the music. She always played an eighties station. Madonna, the queen of the crucifixes, was singing "Borderline."

"Huh?"

"A dress. Did you find one?"

"No." I had forgotten all about it.

"Who's the boy you're going with?" Bebe asked.

"Vic."

"Is he one of those Goth types, like those two guys?"

"Since when do you know about Goth, Mom?" Mina asked.

"Please . . . do you think I was born yesterday? First it was grunge out here. Now Goth. If you ever dress that way, Mina, I'll kill you."

"Great. I'll make sure I dye my hair black and pierce my nose, then."

"Teenagers!" Bebe snapped. She turned up Madonna and sang, while Mina and I groaned in the backseat—Bebe is tone-deaf. After about ten more minutes, Bebe pulled up into my driveway and handed me a bag.

"What's this?"

She wheeled around to look at me before I climbed out of the car. "It's something to wear for homecoming. I'd like to think that if your mother were here, she'd get this for you."

I welled up for a second. "Thanks, Bebe."

"Open it," Bebe said.

I peeked in the bag Bebe had given me. Inside was a little cardboard box. I opened it and lifted up the cotton. There sat a delicate pair of rhinestone earrings, little dangling crosses.

"They're beautiful, Bebe," I said, feeling a lump in my throat.

"You know, I was going to get little rhinestone hearts, but then I saw these, and something told me they were just right for you. I don't know. Maybe it's that cross way up there." She pointed to a cross that hung up high, right in the peak of our roof. We had gargoyles, too, so until my little vampire nightmare I had never given much thought to the cross.

"Bebe, they're very special. Thanks." I leaned

over the seat and gave her a peck on the cheek. Then I climbed out of the car, walked up the steps, and did the whole key ring/lock thing. When I got inside I saw Dad's light on in his study. He was poring over old manuscripts as usual. I walked in, took off my jacket, and kissed him on his cheek. He didn't look up.

"Dad?"

"I'm upset with you, Lucy."

In all my life my father had never been angry with me, and I, in turn, had never been angry with him. I know that sounds ridiculous, since *every* teenager, at some point, hates her parents. But my relationship with Dad was different, given his eccentric behavior. In a way, for a long time I've been acting like the parent. I'm the one who remembers to go grocery shopping (it's not like he'd go to the store anyway) and to make sure we have clean towels and toilet paper in the bathrooms. I do the laundry, and I remind him when it's time to pay the electric bill—I learned to do that after the power company turned off our electricity a time or two.

For the most part he's always trusted me. He's kind of had to. Because he won't leave the house, he's had to accept that what I told him about school or what I was doing was, in fact, true.

"Why are you mad at me?"

"I don't want you having anything to do with Vic Irving. You knew that, and if Carolyn hadn't come here, I think you would have continued lying to me about him. Why?"

"Dad . . . don't you remember what it's like to be sixteen? To like someone so much that when they start walking toward you down the school hallway, you feel like your heart is pounding so loudly everyone can hear it?"

He finally looked at me. "Yes. I felt that way about your mother."

"Then you'd know why I don't want to judge him because his family may or may not be . . . Dad, I can't even say it. Do you know how nuts we sound?"

He nodded. "I do. But I also know vampires are real, Lucy, and you need to be careful. Part of this is my fault. I've been hiding in this house so long. I can't hide anymore. I'm chaperoning that dance. And it's time I told you more about your power. Sit down, sweetie. I guess I'm not so much mad as worried."

I sat down in the big wing-back chair.

"Tell me what happened again with Seth and Jude at the mall."

I repeated the story—what I'd been telling him over the cell phone. This time, of course, I told him

how it ended—with Bebe coming and finding us—
and with me hearing Seth in my head.

"There!"

"There what?"

"That's your power. Your mother's power."

"What? Hearing voices?"

"No. He's drawn to you. Just as Dracula is. The
vampires use their power to mesmerize and control
people. But you can use your powers, if you train
your mind, to draw them to you. If we're smart,
Lucy, we can trap them."

"Trap them?"

He nodded. "The time has come to bring down
the house of Dracula once and for all. At the dance.
You can draw Dracula to you. You'll have to concentrate. But I believe you can do it. And when he shows
up, we'll be waiting for him."

I felt torn. I despised Seth and Jude, but I still
didn't want to believe Vic was like them, too.

"Daddy . . . what about Vic?"

"You know, just as I can relate to being sixteen,
to being crazy about someone, I can also relate to
knowing, deep down, that someone isn't good or
healthy for me. Vic is an Irving, and that means that
even if he hasn't fully turned yet, they're using him
to get to you—and my guess is, he knows it. Lucy,

you have to see that. He can't be oblivious to Seth and Jude."

I nodded. After seeing the kind of power Seth could have over Mina, I knew that even if it hurt, even if it sucked, I would have to break up with Vic.

"Forgive me, Dad? I'm sorry I kind of lied."

"Do you forgive me for hiding from the world all these years?"

I went to him and kissed his cheek. "Of course I do. You're still the dad who tucked me in every night."

He gave me a big hug. Suddenly the phone rang. Dad released me, and I picked up the receiver.

"Hello?"

"Luce, it's Mark." He sounded out of breath.

"What's up?"

"I need you at my house pronto. Faster than pronto."

"Why?"

"It's Jimmy."

"Your little brother?"

"Yeah."

"What about him?"

"Um . . . I think it would be easier to show you."

"Okay . . . I'll be right over."

I hung up the phone. My father asked me what was going on.

"To be honest, Dad, I don't know. Something about Jimmy, Mark's little brother."

"Which one is that?"

The Carnahan family was so big, for most people it was hard to keep them straight.

"The younger one Mark shares a room with."

"The one who hates to shower?"

"Yup." I laughed.

"I hope he's okay."

I nodded. "I'm pretty sure he is. Mark just sounded weird."

I left Dad's study and grabbed a sweatshirt from the hall closet and pulled it on over my head. Then I unlocked the door and dashed out and down the street two doors to the Carnahans'.

The Carnahan house has four bedrooms—not nearly enough. The kids all share bedrooms, and all the bedrooms have at least one set of bunk beds. It would be crowded enough with just the Carnahans, but add the older kids having boyfriends and girl-friends, the younger kids having playmates, Mrs. Carnahan taking care of her mother, and a cousin who was staying with them while her parents were going through a messy divorce, and you have a recipe for sheer chaos. At dinnertime, if you don't grab food fast enough, chances are you're settling for cold cereal.

Mrs. Carnahan is the sweetest lady on the planet. Unlike Bebe, with her stiletto shoes and collagen lips, Mrs. Carnahan pretty much wears Levi's and Mr. Carnahan's old football jerseys from college all the time. I've never seen her with lipstick on, and she usually wears her long hair in a ponytail. She's a little on the chubby side. She says, all the time, "You try popping out nine kids and see if you have a body like Jennifer Aniston."

I walked in through their front door without knocking. No one would ever hear you knock. Too much commotion.

In the living room, poor Mr. Carnahan was trying to watch ESPN. He had the new baby, Jack, on his lap, and two other kids were doing their homework on the coffee table. The cousin, Rebecca, was gabbing on her cell phone, and Nick kept passing through on his in-line skates. Every time he passed, Mr. Carnahan would yell, "No skating in the house," and every time, Nick would grin and ignore him.

Mr. Carnahan owns a garage—he fixes fancy foreign cars, and everyone says he's both the best at what he does, and the only honest mechanic in town.

"Hey, Lucy," he said, glancing over at me.

"Hi, Mr. C."

"Mark's upstairs."

"Okay."

"Take Jack up to Mrs. C, will ya? He needs a diaper change."

Mr. Carnahan held Jack out to me. He's really cute. But at that moment he smelled. Visiting the Carnahans made me *really* certain I wanted to have only one kid when I got married. Two, max. I took Jack in my arms and headed up the stairs. I made a left at the landing and poked my head into Mrs. Carnahan's bedroom.

"Mr. C says Jack needs a change."

She was folding laundry. "What? Are Mr. C's legs broken?" She rolled her eyes. "Good thing I'm still madly in love with that idiot. From the first time I laid eyes on him in college in his football jersey, full head of red hair, to now, pot belly and balding, he's been my guy. All right, hand me the baby."

She reached out her arms for Jack, who squealed with happiness at seeing her, and I gave him to her.

"How'd you know?"

"How'd I know what?"

"That Mr. C was the one for you?"

"I just knew."

"Did you feel like a wreck every time you saw him?"

"Hmm . . . a little. But mostly, when I was around him, I felt like we were the only two people in the entire world."

I tried to think about Vic. Was that the way I felt about him?

"Did your parents like Mr. C?"

"Loved him. He played football for Notre Dame. What's not to love, as my dad used to say."

Somehow, I couldn't imagine Vic being an all-American guy like Mr. C. In fact, every time I thought about Vic lately, I pictured him growing fangs.

Mrs. C changed Jack, singing "You Are My Sunshine" to him. "He likes that. When I sing," she said, looking at me. I walked over and tickled Jack's belly. Sometimes, when I saw Mrs. C, I would get choked up thinking of my own mother. But I think Mrs. C, like Bebe, knew that. Somehow, even with all those kids in that house, there was always an extra hug for me. She scooped Jack up and said, "Let me go return him to the diaper-changing scaredy-cat downstairs."

I wandered out of the bedroom and down the hall to Mark's room. He shares it with Jimmy and also his older brother Tom when Tom is home from college.

"Mark?" I walked in the room.

"Shh!" Mark said.

When I was safely in the room, he shut the door—and locked it. I didn't even know his door had a lock.

"What's going on? I thought you said this was about Jimmy."

"It is. Look!" He held out two glass jars toward me. Both contained bugs. Creepy, crawling bugs.

"Gross!"

"They're Jimmy's."

"You dragged me all the way here—"

"All the way here? It's a thirty-second walk."

"Still, you dragged me here to show me bugs?"

"Yes. I told you, they're Jimmy's."

"So what? Your little brother is disgusting. He picks his nose, won't shower, and watch out if that kid eats baked beans. Collecting bugs? Big deal."

"He eats them."

"What?" I looked at the jar. I'd rather stare down a vampire than eat a bug.

"He *eats* them."

"Gross, even for Jimmy."

"Yes. And so I asked him *why* he was eating bugs.

And he couldn't explain himself. Said he had a dream, and in the dream someone told him to eat bugs, and when he woke up, he couldn't help himself."

"Weird."

"Hello? Earth to Lucy. You reading the *Cliff's Notes* version of *Dracula*?"

"Hmm?"

"Are you not paying attention to the legend? That guy. From the asylum. What's his name? Renfield? The one who eats the bugs. The flies. *Don't you get it*? Don't you remember that part of the book? Dracula's trying to control my little brother."

"But why would he want to control some eleven-year-old kid with body odor?"

"To get to us."

I looked at the jar. Considering how into being gross Jimmy was, it could have been that he was eating bugs for the sheer creep factor of it. But my gut told me that wasn't the reason.

"Damn. You know, Seth and Jude were at the mall today and they made Mina sick. Or at least, Seth did. He was staring at her, like hypnotizing her—my dad called it mesmerizing—and she got physically ill. I think we're going about this vampire thing all wrong."

"What do you mean?"

"We're sitting around waiting for the vampires to make their move. What if we move first?"

"How?"

"We need to find their hangout and get to them somehow."

"How do we do that?"

"I've got a plan. But if we're caught, we're dead."

"You mean the vampires will get us?"

"No. I mean our parents will."

Chapter 17

March 15, 1887

Dearest Diary,

I have been alone since I left Europe. Most especially, I have been alone since I escaped Misters Irving and Stoker. I stay few places very long, moving from town to city to town, never giving my real name, trying to find employment as a governess.

Three months ago, however, I met a man named John Goode. He's quite tall and handsome, and he is a bit of an adventurer, having made his fortune owning several trading posts and then a general store. He's a fine catch, as Mrs. MacDonald would say. However, I think she eyed Mr. Goode for her sister, Annabelle, and most certainly not for her lowly governess.

When I first laid eyes on John, dare I call him "my John," I felt the earth move. After being so

135

tired, so weary, for so long—going without sleep, suffering from nightmares and visions—conversing with him made me feel as if all were right with the world again. He came calling soon thereafter. I would find that my hours with him passed so quickly that I would hardly notice the passage of time at all.

He proposed to me last Saturday. He is quite an adventurer, and he envisions us traveling north and seeking further fortunes.

I told him, however, that I would have to consider his proposal. He asked me if it was that I didn't love him. Nothing, of course, could be farther from the truth. I love him as I love life. I love him with the whole of my tired heart. For that reason, I wonder if I can bring him into the strange tale and saga of Mr. Stoker and Mr. Irving. Would John even believe me? I don't know if I believe myself. I only know what I have seen and what I have felt.

I would rather die than place John in jeopardy. I would rather die than live without him. What shall I do, dear diary? What shall I do?

I need protection. I feel sheltered and safe when I am within John's arms, but is it fair to bring him into a life of danger? I pray I make the right decision. I'm so tired of being alone, a woman without a home, without a moment's rest.

Good-night, Dear Diary,

Lucy

Chapter 18

Thursday night, Mina told her parents she was sleeping at my house to work on our term paper. A term paper that did not exist.

Mark told his mother that he was sleeping at my house because Jimmy smelled so bad he couldn't take another night in their room until Jimmy bathed. She bought that excuse. I would, too. So would anyone who smelled Jimmy. The Carnahans tend not to freak out over what they call "phases"—and Jimmy smelling was one of them. Still, Mr. and Mrs. C didn't have to share a room with the little stinker.

I told my father I was sleeping at Mina's house because Bebe wanted to give us both makeovers. Also entirely believable. I once came home from Mina's with false eyelashes sitting like hairy caterpillars on my eyes.

Instead, the three of us met at the Burger Barn, this place that served "the Fattest Burgers in Seattle"—with big, thick milk shakes Mark loved. In the Burger Barn restrooms, Mark, Mina, and I went in as ordinary-looking teens. We came out looking Goth. Not just Goth. We came out looking like we ruled the underworld kingdom of Goth. I had on pale white makeup and dark black eyeliner, with a black leather jacket, black tights, Doc Martens, and black lipstick. Mina had spiked her hair with gel, and wore enough eyeliner to obscure her pretty green eyes. Mark spiked his hair and also wore eyeliner—we made him—and he had on black jeans and a black T-shirt. We had bought an assortment of fake piercings at a novelty jewelry store. In short, we looked fierce.

All the better, of course, to go to the Underground, the club where Jude had gone the night of my date with Vic.

Mina has a weekly allowance that matches my yearly allowance, not to mention her own credit card, so she hired us a cab to get to the club. Mark and Mina were my best friends, and I didn't even recognize them. I swear, if I had walked into a bar and seen the two of them—had *tripped* over the two of them—I wouldn't have known who they were. I was counting on this as we went in search of Seth and Jude.

Mark was the king of the illegal ID. As a Carnahan, there was an unwritten advantage. Mr. and Mrs. Carnahan may have had nine kids, but Mr.

Carnahan had six brothers and four sisters. Each of them had a large family, all of which meant that Mark had seventy-eight first cousins. *Seventy-eight!* I wasn't sure how he even remembered all of their first names. However, all those kids—a lot of them older than we are—meant that there was an abundance of licenses to borrow, hence fake IDs. The rules to borrowing a Carnahan fake ID were:

1 If you get sloppy drunk and spew bodily fluids of any sort at any time during your possession of the fake ID, you will never be allowed to borrow it again.

2 If you are arrested while in possession of said fake ID, not only will you never be allowed to borrow the ID again, but all Carnahans will close ranks and issue a denial of the knowledge of your exploits—you're on your own.

3 Don't get caught by a parent, or unseen, slow, torturous death awaits you.

Mark was "Atticus Carnahan." He hated being Atticus—a cousin named for the character of Atticus Finch in *To Kill a Mockingbird*. Nonetheless, most Carnahans resemble one another, and in this case he looked a lot like his cousin Atticus. Mina was "Casey Carnahan," and I was "Anna Maria Carnahan." Of course, none of us looked like the pictures on the licenses. I mean, if we weren't dripping in eyeliner and greased spiked hair, we might have. So I hoped the bouncers were easygoing.

In the back of the cab, we checked our weapons—spray bottles of vampire repellent and neon-plastic squirt guns of holy water. Mark's mother had bottles of water from Lourdes and various Catholic holy places—one of her aunts was a nun who gave them as Christmas gifts. We felt bad about doing it, but Mark replaced the holy water with tap water, and then filled the water pistols. I wasn't thinking we'd *kill* the vampires—and can you *kill* someone already undead?—so much as make them really, really sick. I figured maybe that way they'd know to leave us alone.

The cab left us off in front of the Underground. I may live in the Munster house, and maybe I don't scare easily, but I felt in over my head with one look at the Underground. Everyone waiting to get inside was pierced just about anywhere you could be. A few guys had spikes inserted *under* the skin of their bald heads, so that they looked like spiny lizards.

I've always wanted a tattoo. Something small and tasteful—maybe the Chinese symbol for dream.

But the patrons of the Underground took tattooing to a new level. Women and men were inked from head to toe; some of the guys—and girls—with bald heads had whole elaborate scenes in vivid ink on their skulls.

Some of the designs were typical—Asian symbols, Harley wings, names, roses, daggers, and flags. But as we stood in line, I also saw a few that unnerved me. Drops of blood, images of vampires, bats, wolves, and words in Latin or Greek. Words that looked at least a little familiar from my father's books.

We reached the bouncer, who didn't give our licenses more than a perfunctory glance. "Five-buck cover charge," he said monotonously. Mark pulled a twenty out of his pocket and paid. And we entered into the club, the doorway to a world dark and sinister that the rest of Pacific Cedar knew nothing about. We lived our lives oblivious to the evil around us. My father was right. My mother was right. Once you know the undead are part of our world, you start to see shadows everywhere.

Now, Mina, Mark, and I were about to see the truth. There would be no turning back, no hiding.

We were entering the realm of darkness.

Chapter 19

The Underground had three levels. On the first floor were several bars and a dance floor. The second level had couches—and as we walked along in the moody darkness, we noticed the couches were most definitely being used for sex. The top floor was live music.

"Crap," Mina said when we got to the top level. "It's Jude's band."

Vic had a band, too. Mostly he played coffee-houses where the acoustic-guitar rock-folk he played was a big hit. Jude's band played this dark, Goth-inspired metal stuff.

"Mina," I shouted over the music, "remember what I said."

"Yes. Believe in them and protect against them in my mind."

"You need to think defensively. Say something like a mantra over and over in your mind. Like, 'You shall not have me, you shall not have me.'"

"Or what about, 'Screw off, vampire boy, Screw off, vampire boy,'" Mark offered.

"Nice, Mark," I rolled my eyes at him.

"That's Atticus to you."

The three of us started laughing.

"What, exactly, are we trying to do here?" Mina asked.

"Just stick to the plan. We stay together. Mark, I don't care what you say—if you have to pee, you're coming in the girls' room."

"It's unisex here anyway," he said.

"Fine. But whatever happens, we don't get separated. We try to blend in. But mostly we're looking for vampires. This is where they hang out. You guys have your camera phones?"

They both nodded.

"All right then, you snap anyone you think is a vampire—but don't let them see you. We'll make our own chart and compare it to Mr. Dobbs's. The idea is to take down the top guy."

"And what if Seth or Jude tries to attack us? This isn't as safe as the mall," Mina said.

"True, but we're as smelly as possible with the vampire repellent."

"When is your uncle going to make me a cologne?"

"Soon, Mark, I promise."

I handed each of them a small vial of the vampire poison, a pure version of garlic oil, sulfur, and other compounds that my godfather and father swore could kill a vampire. "This is for emergencies."

"Okay," said Mina, taking her vial. "So I slip this in the drink of any vampire. But what if we make a mistake? What if it's just some Goth person and not a vampire?"

"They'll get an upset stomach, but in a day or so they'll be fine."

"But to a vampire it's deadly, right?" Mark asked.

"I think so."

"You *think* so?" Mina shrieked over the music. "You *think* so? You drag us to a club filled with vampires and vampire lovers, as well as just ordinary scary humans, and you tell us you 'think' the vial can kill them?"

"Well, it's not like my father has some steady supply of vampires to try it out on. But it should work. Now, let's go scope out the club."

I looked around the top floor. "Notice anything?" I asked Mina and Mark.

"What?" Mina asked.

"Look at them all."

They looked at the crowd listening to the music. "My God," Mina said. "Was that how I was?"

"Yeah. Just as bad or worse."

The crowd was mesmerized by Jude. I've been to rock concerts where everyone sort of gets into this groove, rocking to the same song or sound, but this was different. This was mass hypnosis or something. It was like they were all drugged and robotic. All focusing their minds and energy on one man—Jude.

We went down the stairs and started on the ground floor. We tried to fit in, not looking surprised at the fevered pitch of the dancers, who really got into the music so much it seemed like a religious experience, almost. People ground into one another, with guys sliding their hands up the tops of girls, feeling their breasts, and girls writhing down the front of the guys they were dancing with. Sometimes women danced together, or a mixed group of guys and girls clustered, forming this mini mosh pit.

Mina held one of Mark's hands. I held the other. I tried to look stone-faced, scary, tough. The music was so loud, I felt it in my belly.

Then I saw him. Seth. He was making his way toward us, focusing on Mina.

"Start saying your mantra, Mina."

I watched her move her lips, repeating something to herself over and over.

"Mark, you take Mina on the dance floor. Wrap your arms around her. Hold her close to you."

He nodded.

"What about you?" Mina asked. "We're supposed to stick together."

"I'll be fine." I heard my mother's voice, her words echoing from the diary and into my soul. *You are far stronger than you realize, Lucy.*

I felt Seth behind me, and then he put his lips to the back of my neck. I started and wheeled around, feeling the spot where he kissed me and pulling my hand to the front of my face, making sure there was no blood.

"What do you want?" I snapped at him.

"Her," he said ominously, jerking his head toward Mina.

"Well, you can't have her."

"I can if I get rid of you."

I felt a chill pass over me. Instinctively I put my hand in the front of my skirt pocket and touched the vial, which I hid in the palm of my hand. Then I put my hands behind my back, uncapping it slowly.

"We're all around, you know. You just need to

take off those blinders you wear. Then you'll see you're fighting a losing battle."

"I don't want to fight you. I just want you to leave me alone."

"Sorry. Too late for that. A century or two of history . . . Now shut your eyes, Lucy, and when you open them again, see with the eyes of your great-great-grandmother."

I closed my eyes for just a second, and when I opened them the club was transformed. It was still the same club, same music. There were Mina and Mark dancing close together, but I could *see* the vampires in a way I hadn't been able to before. Some of them could cling to the walls, and they all had a strange paleness to them, beyond even the paleness of the makeup and style of the Goth partyers. When they breathed, some of them had clouds of condensation around them, as if they were so cold that mingling with the heat of the dancers caused a reaction.

I looked at the mouths of dancers, writhing in the throes of some new dance move. I saw flashes of fangs. The vampires were all around. They were a part of the club.

I looked at a bartender. He bared his teeth. I needed to get Mina and Mark and get out of there. I made a move to go on the dance floor.

"Not so fast." Seth came close to me and hissed in my ear.

I didn't have a very good feeling about any of this. I realized now that my plan was a weak one. We wanted to show them we weren't afraid, get them sick, burn them with holy water. But I hadn't counted on there being so many of them. It was three of us and, by the looks of it, dozens of them.

I took the vial and said a silent prayer; then I flung its contents in Seth's face. His reaction was intense. He squealed a high-pitched shriek, which seemed to alert every other vampire in the place that something was wrong. He shrank back from me, gasping and clutching his sides, then covering his eyes.

"You bitch!" he yelled at me. "You won't live until tomorrow."

By now, Mina and Mark realized that some of the dancers were reacting to what was going on between Seth and me. Mina and Mark came over to me, and I shouted, "We've got to get out of here. They're everywhere."

With me leading the way, the three of us pushed and maneuvered our way through the crowded club. I had Mina spraying perfume around us as we walked, like a perpetual vampire-repellent cloud.

We had out our plastic water guns and squirted

holy water all around us. Vampires hissed, but shrank back from us. I blasted one female vampire in the face, and holy water got in her mouth. She fell to the floor, throwing up and writhing right there in front of everyone.

My heart pounded in time to the music, it seemed. Vampires were right here, among the club-goers. I wondered if people could tell the difference. It was almost impossible to, but now that my eyes had been opened, my world would never be the same.

"Oh, my God!" I screamed as we got to the exit. Looking over my shoulder I saw three vampires closing in on us. They were going to follow us out into the night—and we still needed a cab.

"We're going to be vampire food," Mark wailed. He turned around and squirted his water gun. His plastic gun was lime green. I didn't imagine there were too many vampire slayers with plastic water guns. The vampires stayed back a little, shrieking, but then Mark was out of holy water.

"Damn! I'm out of ammunition!"

I wheeled around and started firing my gun. I got one of them right in the eye, and it literally started smoking, steam coming out as the eyeball burned as if it had been touched by acid.

"Crap!" I said. "That's going to make him mad. God, that's disgusting."

Mina grabbed my hand, and we pushed open the heavy club doors. Outside on the sidewalk people were milling around. I hoped that we would be safe as long as there were witnesses, but something told me these guys didn't care.

Sure enough, they were out of the club a moment behind us, and walked in our direction.

I looked up and down the street. Typical. Can't find a cab when you need one.

Suddenly a somewhat beat-up looking gray car pulled up right at the curb where we were standing. The passenger door flung open, and a man leaned across from the driver's side.

"Get in!"

We didn't need to be asked twice.

But I had a lot of questions.

Just how had Mr. Dobbs found us?

Chapter 20

Are you three out of your minds? You must be, you know, if you went there, of all places. And I must be out of my mind for bringing you all home. I could lose my teaching license."

"We won't tell anyone; we swear," Mina said. Her knees were shaking, and she put her hands on top of them to try to make them stop.

Mina and Mark were in the backseat, and I was in the front. I looked over at Mr. Dobbs as he drove. "What's with that club?"

"You tell me."

"I saw vampires. Lots of them."

He nodded. "You never should have gone there."

The words came tumbling out in a jumble. "But Seth had mind-controlled Mina, and now Jimmy is eating bugs, and Mina saw a wolf in her backyard, and—"

"Hold on." Mr. Dobbs lifted one hand from the wheel and made a sort of "stop" gesture. "Hold on.

I'm not saying that in theory, your idea to go there wasn't a good one. It's one I tried myself."

"What do you mean?"

"You wanted to confront them."

I nodded. "I wanted to make them leave us alone. I thought if I could make them see I wasn't afraid of them that they would leave, would stop following us. We came armed with a garlic poison, holy water—and let me tell you, if you've never seen an eyeball disintegrate, it's beyond gross. Anyway, we wanted to make them ill. We wanted to show them we're onto them and we're not afraid of confronting them—even though deep down we are."

"But they're not reasonable, Lucy. You're thinking like a human being. You have something they no longer have."

"What?"

"A soul."

I shivered a little bit at the thought.

"You know, Lucy, my family thinks I'm crazy. I've been hunting vampires since I was your age. But I've also spent my whole life immersed in world religions—figuring that would have some secrets to combating the soulless. I'm a Buddhist, but I appreciate Judaism, Islam, Christianity . . . as well as many, many minor religions most people know nothing about. And the soul is something universal. We all, or most of us, believe there's a fundamental something to us, an essence that carries on after we die. But vampires forfeit that soul. So reasoning with them is like reasoning with a sociopath."

Mark leaned over from the backseat. "There were so many of them."

"Seattle is a mecca for them. The Goth scene lets them blend in. L.A. has a pretty high population—but then again, the entertainment business is naturally bloodsucking. They don't cluster in small towns. They go to places they won't stick out so much, places with clubs that stay open all night long. Like London, New York. Places where people can vanish from the street and no one will notice."

"People would notice if I disappeared," I said.

"Sure. But sadly in any big city there are runaways, homeless, addicts. They're the unseen. They're our version of the untouchables in India. Let me ask you something. Did you have to look at the vampires in a different way in order to really see them?"

I nodded.

"Well, same with the unseen people. Look around." As he said this, we drove by a street with two homeless people lying on the sidewalk. "The vampires see them. They see the people society throws away as useless or unworthy. To vampires they're food, sustenance, blood."

"And that club? They all like to go there?" Mina asked.

"It's owned by Dracula himself."

"What?" I asked.

"Vic and Jude's great-great-grandfather."

"I thought vampires couldn't have children," Mark said.

"Before he allowed himself to be turned fully, before he accepted his role in the lineage, he fathered two sons, and they've gone on to do the same. The old man is still alive, but he doesn't look it. Vic and Jude may even think he's just their grandfather. Or they may know the truth. It seems that, like your mother, the age of sixteen is when the family reveals its secrets."

I shook my head. "So how do we defeat them?"

"Not with getups like those," he said, looking in the rearview mirror at Mina and Mark and then at me. "You guys look much better in your regular attire. Mark, I even miss your usual T-shirt."

Mark has this quirky thing about always wearing a Notre Dame T-shirt—his dad's alma mater.

"Notre Dame doesn't quite fit in with the whole Goth look," Mark joked.

"Well, guys, I have a better idea. You need to fight them on your territory. You need to lure them to a place where you feel comfortable."

"The homecoming dance," I said. "We could bring them there, and then trap them somehow."

"Too risky."

"It can work. I just know it."

"Well, we'd have to do a lot of planning. And we'd have to be careful. It could all blow up in our faces," Mr. Dobbs said.

"We will. We'll plan it down to the last detail. Garlic punch and all."

Of course, not everything goes according to plan. . . .

Chapter 21

We had Mr. Dobbs drop the three of us off at the Carnahans'. One thing about their house—a couple of extra people and no one notices. We scrubbed and scrubbed at our faces and each took a long shower; then we all crashed in the living room on the couches—which was better than bunking in with Mark's smelly, insect-eating brother. The next day I went home and Vic called me.

"What the hell is wrong with you, Lucy?"

"What do you mean?"

"I mean Jude told me you showed up at the club and started trouble."

"He's full of it. I didn't start trouble . . . I just . . . went there with my friends. Um, to hang out."

I heard him sort of laugh, only it sounded more menacing. "Since when are you into the Goth scene, little Miss Perfect?"

"Little Miss Perfect? What's that supposed to mean?"

"Nothing," he snapped.

"Vic? What's wrong with you?" The whole time I'd known Vic, we'd never really fought.

"Look, keep away from my brother."

"Why?"

"Just do what I said, Lucy!"

"You know, I don't like being told what to do."

"Well, get used to it."

"No, I think *you'd* better get used to not being with me."

"What about the homecoming dance?"

"Find someone more your type. You know . . . without a pulse."

I slammed down the phone. Vic had turned sixteen two months before I did. He was becoming a vampire. I couldn't prove it, but I felt it. I felt sorry for him a little. I thought about my father. He would do anything for me—even come out of the house for the first time in ten years. I know he had my best interests at heart all the time, every minute of every day.

No, I wasn't Little Miss Perfect. I didn't live in the perfect house. I didn't have the perfect family— mom, dad, 2.3 kids, and a dog. I had a cat who used to be a human, a kooky father, and a gargoyle above my door. But compared to Vic? My life was sunshine.

Chapter 22

In the interest of defeating the vampires and getting rid of Seth and his Mina obsession, I turned to my mother's diary. I wasn't the first Lucy to want to kill a vampire. And my guess was, I wouldn't be the last person to try either.

But it seems my mom had help in her quest. Professor V.

> *Dear Lucy,*
>
> *Let me tell you about Professor Von Helsing.*
>
> *When your father and I met him, we were just dating. I loved your father very much, but I have to confess that I found Professor V really dashing. He had long, flowing black hair with just a little curl at the collar, and he always dressed in jeans, boots, and a white shirt and blazer. He spoke as many languages as your father. And he was an expert on vampires.*

In fact, he was the only person I'd ever met who had actually killed one.

We were in London when we met. Your father and I were visiting an old library in search of a specific ancient text. Well, so was Professor V. When we went to introduce ourselves, he stuck his hand out to me, and said, "I already know—Lucy, right?"

Of course, I found this odd, even a little bit scary. I smiled and said, "How do you know?"

"You look just like your great-greatgrandmother, the actress. And you're here researching vampires, aren't you?"

The three of us left the library and found a little pub, where we sat for hours and hours and talked—your father and I told him what we knew. Professor V told us what he knew.

This diary, Lucy, and all the books on vampire myths that fill your father's study, they're nothing compared to Professor V's wealth of knowledge. It's unbelievable. He was the great-grandson of the inspiration for Stoker's Professor Van Helsing. The family hadn't even changed their name; they were all so defiant, so brave. Maybe, your father says, so foolhardy.

Professor V had personally killed a dozen vampires—the old-fashioned way. He would find them as they slept by day and drive a stake through their heart. His stakes weren't wooden—they were titanium mixed with silver, and he had them specially made. He wasn't taking any chances.

After talking to Professor V, I realized I was in way over my head. Your father and I begged him to come back to America with us. He agreed. He packed his bags and his passport, and he was on a plane inside of two weeks.

Those were the happiest days of my life— except, of course, once you came along, darling. Your father and Professor V became best friends, despite the fact that we all knew that V, as we called him, loved me a little, too. This was never spoken of, though. Your father understood that he was the one for me, my darling, slightly absentminded genius, and V would just say to him, "You lucky bastard," with that British accent of his.

We spent our days working on our research and our evenings talking. Your father and I married, and V was the best man.

Dearest V was living with us, but he felt that maybe three was a crowd, and he eventually fell in love and got married. His wife's name was Ophelia, and she was the daughter of a boat captain who did whale tours off the coast here. She was a creature of the sea—not a mermaid, but a girl who lived for the water. She and V lived in a small house on an island that you had to take a ferry to get to.

One night he showed up here at our house with a warning that Dracula was closing in. His face was pale and drawn. By this time you were little, and I was sick. We hadn't told him, but he took one look at me and knew. He was so distraught he went out into the dark night and somehow found and battled the dark one. He showed up here, deeply wounded. Mortally wounded, I thought. Your father and I brought him inside and tended to him. The next day Professor V as you know and see him as a cat was lying on the bed. Until we kill Dracula, he will remain in that form.

Your father and I felt it was our duty to go tell Ophelia about what had happened to her husband. But since he had kept his relationship with her so private, we had no idea what she did and did not know about vampires and our secrets. I suppose it was cowardly of us. I'm sure she thinks he ran off. In retrospect, I just wouldn't have known what to say to her.

I only wish Professor V were here in his old form. Because I think he's really the only one who can kill Dracula. I write you this, my darling, because you need to know that battling Dracula won't be easy. Your mind needs to be strong. If you confront him, you need to be sure that you're ready. Be strong, Lucy. And know I am with you in spirit.

Love,
Mom

Chapter 23

I went on my computer and did a search for Ophelia Van Helsing. I found her address. She no longer lived on an island, but was in Seattle, down by the wharves.

On Saturday I told my dad that I was going to Mina's, and instead I took a bus downtown and eventually found Ophelia's house.

The house was small and wooden and was built into the hillside. It overlooked the water, and at the top of it was a widow's walk. I wondered if she went up there to look for the dashing Professor V.

I had stuck the diary in my backpack, but I couldn't imagine her believing a word of what I was about to say. "Hello, ma'am. You don't know me, but my cat is your late husband, Professor Van Helsing." Yeah, right.

But I also wondered if maybe Professor V had left behind some papers, some journal of his own that would offer more clues as to how to kill Dracula. It was a long shot, but one worth taking.

I climbed the steep wooden steps to the front door. With every breath, condensation swirled around my mouth. It was chilly, and I wrapped my scarf tighter around my neck.

I rang the doorbell. No one came. I rang again. Still no answer, so I knocked and then sat down on the top step. I was willing to wait all day for Ophelia.

"Can I help you?"

I turned around at the sound of a man's voice. He was at the window, and I couldn't see him quite well.

"I'm looking for Ophelia Van Helsing."

"Hold on."

I stood up when I heard someone fiddling with the locks on the door. As the door swung open, I found myself face-to-face with the hottest guy I'd ever seen in my life. He looked like how my mother described Professor V. He had dark curly hair, dark brown eyes, and he was really tall and very well built. His hair was messed up in a sexy kind of way. I could barely speak.

"Um . . . Is Mrs. Van Helsing here?" I felt like I could barely squeak out the words.

"No. She's out on a whale watching trip. She won't be back for a week."

"Oh." Now what?

"Can I help you?"

"I don't think so."

"I'm her son," he offered. "Christopher Van Helsing."

Yeah. Your father is a cat.

"Lucy." I stuck my hand out. "Lucy Hellenberg."

"I thought so," he said, and smiled. He had two deep dimples in his cheeks.

"You know me?"

"Not exactly. My father had a picture of your mother, and you look just like her. Do you want to come in?"

I nodded.

He ushered me into the small house. The sea was a huge part of it—shells and sea glass, wind chimes, and driftwood-lined shelves. Pictures of whales and the ocean were framed on the walls. It even smelled of the sea.

"Do you want something to drink?"

I shook my head no.

"If you're here looking for my father, he left long before I was born." Christopher sat down on the couch and gestured for me to sit down in an armchair. He looked two or three years older than I.

"Oh, no, I wasn't here to look for him exactly."

"Then why are you here?"

I bit my lip.

"Tell me. Please . . . do you know what happened to him?" His voice was hopeful, anxious.

"Um, what do you know about your father's work? Did he leave any papers behind?"

"I know about my father." Christopher's voice was quiet. "He was a vampire hunter."

There. It was out in the open.

"And what do you think about that?" I asked. "Do you think he was crazy?"

"My mother used to. She wouldn't talk about him. But eventually I found all his books and papers up in the attic. She said she assumed something terrible happened to him. But she was never sure whether or not to believe in all of it."

"Do you believe?"

Christopher nodded. "I've spent the last three years learning all I can about his legacy. The more I learned, the more I saw. It was like before I used to see things, but now I see what's *really* there. Like vampires. They're all around us."

I felt a flood of relief course through me. That was exactly how I felt. Finally, a kindred spirit.

"They are. And they're after me, just like they were after my mother and grandmother and great-grandmother and Lucy Barrows. And I'm just tired of the people I love, like my dad, being afraid. And

167

I'm tired of vampires bothering my friends and the people I care about. And I want to end it. I want to get Dracula once and for all. It's just that I'm not sure how. I mean, my father and I have this plan to lure him to me, and we know about garlic poison and stakes through the heart. But I also know how powerful he is, and I'm not sure I'm ready. My mother left behind a diary for me. She told me I really had to be sure I was prepared. I have to be so careful."

"I would, too, after what he did to your mother."

Suddenly the room seemed twenty degrees colder. I felt sick to my stomach.

"What do you mean?"

"I mean how she died."

"My mother had leukemia. She got sick and died."

"Is that what your father told you?"

I felt like I was going to throw up. Part of me didn't want to hear what Christopher was going to say next.

"Yes, that's what my dad told me."

"Come on," he said very gently. He held out his hand. "I want to show you my father's papers."

I put my hand in his, and I swear it was as if I had been holding his hand my whole life. I wanted to kiss him. How crazy was that? I was learning about my mother's death with a strange guy I barely knew. A strange guy I wanted to kiss.

Christopher led me up the stairs to an attic room set up like an office or a study.

"This is where he used to do his work. They moved here from the island. He was worried about my mother being alone on the island when he would go to hunt vampires."

I took a deep breath. I could almost feel the presence of Professor V. Could picture him in my mind looking out over the sea as he pored over his books.

Christopher led me to a big oak desk, and on top of it was a thick leather book, almost as thick as a Bible. Christopher sat down and started leafing through pages. Eventually he found what he was looking for.

She is sick. I don't think she's even told David, but I know. She can't hide it from me. I love her. It's a different love than I feel for Ophelia. My Ophelia is the sea and life and a quiet respite from my relentless hunt. But Lucy, she's like a sister, and yet not. We can't hide anything from each other. She was bitten.

I see the tiny scar on her neck. I don't know when it happened, but it did. She has the hall-marks of leukemia, a blood disorder. But I know its origins lie with him. He bit her. And if it's the last thing I do, I will kill him as he sleeps.

"Does my father know?"

"Yeah. Later on, my father writes that your mother finally told your dad. There was no cure, though she had time yet—it was a lingering illness. My father disappeared a short time later."

I felt like crying, and tears started streaming down my face. Christopher put his arms around me. It was odd, but I felt like I had always known him.

He leaned his chin on top of my head and whispered, "Shh . . . it's okay. I know how you feel."

I looked up at him. Here was one person in the entire world who could understand what I'd been through. Who knew what it was like to lose a parent to Dracula. Who knew what it was like to see the world, not with rose-colored glasses, but with seeing eyes that showed all the shadows and darkness. I stared into his eyes. He had been hugging me, comforting me. Now he put a hand on each side of my face and tilted my face upward more. He leaned closer to me and kissed me, softly nibbling on my bottom lip.

Now, I've kissed Vic, and I've kissed Mark once, a long time ago when we were stupid enough to think maybe we should try dating—it was a disaster. I kissed this guy named Zachary whom I met one summer at a concert I went to with Mina. And I kissed a couple of random guys at parties here and there—not very often. But this kiss made me really, actually, truly go weak in the knees.

He kissed me harder, and soon we were pressed against each other really tight. Finally he pulled away and then kissed two salty tears that were left on my face.

I was speechless. Nothing like this had ever happened to me. I was connected to him—and I forgot all about Vic, all about my problems. I just felt something bigger than I was.

"God," he said. "I didn't mean to do that. I . . . Wow." He exhaled.

Wow pretty much summed it up for me, too.

"Lucy, I'm sorry about your mother. But I'm glad you found me."

"Me, too. Um . . . okay, I know this sounds insane, but I brought my mother's diary to show you. Now, however weird you think your father's papers are, I've got something huge to show you. Wait here."

I went back downstairs and collected my backpack. I brought it upstairs to the attic and took out her journal. I found the spot about Professor V.

"Your cat?" He looked at me incredulously after he'd read it. Then I told him the story about Vic and Seth and Jude and Professor V attacking Vic's face.

"You have a boyfriend?"

I shook my head. "It was sort of that way, but then all this totally weird stuff started happening. We broke up. He's related to the Irvings."

I told him about the club and about all the vampires. And about Mr. Dobbs and his attempts to help us.

"A cat."

I nodded. "He's an awesome cat. Very distinguished."

Christopher looked at me and smiled. "You know, you're probably the only person on this entire planet I can talk to about this stuff."

"If we kill Dracula, your father can take human form again."

"Easier said than done."

"We were planning on trying to get him at homecoming."

"Which you're going to with this Vic guy."

"Um, not anymore," I said. "It was before I totally realized what was going on. I'll just go with Mina and Mark—my two best friends."

"Mina?"

"Yeah, I know." I rolled my eyes. "I don't know how I missed all these clues in my life before."

"So we get them at the homecoming dance then."

I nodded. He said *we*. I was relieved. There was a quiet strength about him. He was a Van Helsing. He would have to know as much about vampire slaying as I did.

"I just want to get Dracula. Maybe if I do, maybe if we kill him, not only would your father return to human form, but maybe Vic and Jude could have a chance at a normal life. Seth, too. Maybe they will be turned back to normal."

It wasn't that I wanted Vic back, or even that I cared about Jude and Seth, but a part of me was sad that their lives were being ruined by Dracula, too. Just in a different way.

I heard the sound of dog paws on the wooden steps. A minute or two later a huge white dog came into the attic.

"What kind of dog is that?"

"She's no dog," Christopher said. "She's a wolf." He put his palm out and the wolf came over and licked it. "Kayla's a beauty, and she and I have spent years training. She's descended from a tough line, and she's going to challenge Dracula in his wolf form."

"You're sure she can?"

He nodded. "She was my father's companion when he and my mother lived on the island. She never left his side. My mother said when my father disappeared, the wolf lay on the steps waiting for him every day for two years. By the time I was walking and talking, she became my defender. She loved my father. She loves me. It's as if she was born to help us. She's fearless."

Outside the attic window, I could see storm clouds gathering over the water.

"Storm coming," I whispered.

Christopher came up behind me.

"Nothing like listening to the rain hit the roof."

The two of us went and sat down on an old couch and waited for the storm. The hair on the back of my neck stood on end as the air grew electric from the coming lightning and thunder. We talked quietly all afternoon, stopping to kiss every few minutes, as the rain pelted the roof and made us feel like we were in our own little cocoon.

The white wolf curled up at our feet. Every once in a while she lifted her head to look at us. Then she would lower it again. But she never seemed to rest. Not really. It was as if she was guarding us against anything that blew in with the storm.

Chapter 24

Dear Diary,

I'm in love.

I spent the whole day with Christopher. I am in love. Officially, really, truly.

You know, I've felt like the outsider, the weird girl, my whole life. When everyone else at school had a mom and a dad at school plays and on special occasions, I was the girl with no one. Actually, that's not true. Sweet Mrs. Carnahan always pretended I was just one more in their huge family. But still, I felt alone in a way. Until today.

Do you know what it's like to meet someone and feel like you've known them forever? That's how I feel with him. He understands all of the bizarre things that have been happening lately. It's like I was born to be with him. He doesn't think my life is nuts. He doesn't think this old Munster house is all that weird.

Everything my mother said about Professor V is true about his son. He's very sexy and has this way about him. And then some. After we'd spent all day listening to the rain, he drove me back home—he's almost nineteen and has a license! His wolf's name is Kayla, and she came in the car with us. She never leaves his side.

When we got to my house, he came in and met my father. I don't think Dad was thrilled that I had gone off on my own yet again, but he was so grateful to be able to meet Christopher. He and my mom hadn't known Ophelia had been pregnant when Professor V turned feline.

Professor V walked over and purred. I keep thinking, wouldn't it be great if he could be his old self again and go back to Ophelia and Christopher?

Anyway, we're still formulating our plans. When I showed Christopher out, we stood on the porch and made out for an hour. I know I liked Vic, but this is different. Now all I have to do is make sure we can avoid all the vampires, kill Dracula, rescue Jimmy from bug eating, stop the mind control, and live happily ever after.

Yeah, right.

That stuff only happens in the movies.

Chapter 25

Dad?"

It was way after midnight, and Dad was still working in his study.

"Yeah, Luce?"

"How come you never told me how Mom really died?"

He put down his pen and stared off into space.

"Dad?"

"It's hard to say, Luce. For a long time I thought I was protecting you. Parents do it all the time. We think you're too young to handle something, and then lo and behold, you're too old *not* to tell you the truth, but by then we've been telling the fairy tale for so long, we don't know how to undo it."

"Did she suffer?"

"A bit. Yeah. It was before you were born, Lucy. Before you were even a twinkle in our eyes, as they say. She wanted to go investigate a sighting of a strange wolf in the park that we read about in the paper. She was like you, Luce. A bit headstrong. She'd get an idea and go off and do it on her own. Fearless, maybe a little less cautious than she needed to be."

I nodded, feeling like I was going to cry, thinking about her.

"She didn't tell me. Not until much, much later. She was at the park, it was daytime, but it was so overcast that it seemed like night, or at least dusk. She was attacked by Dracula. He appeared out of the fog and bit her neck. He wasn't able to turn her. A busload of sightseers and a police car on patrol both arrived at the park. Dracula disappeared before he could kill her, but the bite was serious. He's powerful enough that . . . he couldn't have fed on her blood for more than a couple of seconds, but that was enough to make her sick."

"Couldn't you . . . I don't know, treat it?"

He shook his head. "He didn't turn her and he didn't kill her, so she just grew weaker and weaker. Like I said, she didn't tell me at first. She would just tire a little easier. Then, when she was pregnant with you, it manifested as severe anemia. She was taking iron—the doctor prescribed strong iron pills—but they didn't help all that much. The vampire disease progressed. By the time she told me what had happened, the doctors thought she had all the hallmarks of leukemia—but she wouldn't respond to traditional treatment. As she grew weaker, she was determined to leave you that diary, to leave you her legacy."

"I wish I could remember her better."

"She was something, Lucy. As spunky as you. She was exactly the type of girl who would do something like take a bus to go find Ophelia."

"Sorry about that," I said sheepishly. "I just had to find out about Professor V."

"And instead you found Christopher."

I flushed. "You can tell, huh?"

He nodded. "There's something between the two of you. Reminds me of the day a beautiful black-haired girl came barging into my office asking me if I could translate an old manuscript for her."

"Do you think a girl like me can get her happy ending, Dad?"

"A girl like you?"

"You know, the girl everyone feels sorry for."

"Oh . . . you mean the girl in the Munsters' house with the father who won't come outside?"

I nodded.

"Sure, he whispered. "Girls like that can have happy endings, same as everyone else."

✳

Homecoming was a week away. And Mina and I were shopping for dresses. She was going as Mark's date—only they told everyone, "It's not really a date!"

"Let me get this straight," she said. "You and Christopher talk on the phone every night until one in the morning."

"Yeah."

"And you're absolutely in love with him."

"Yeah."

"And you're pretty sure he's equally crazy about you."

"Yeah. He says he can't sleep, can't eat, can't think."

"Sounds like love. Or maybe the flu."

"Very funny, Mina."

"So he has the love flu, but he's not going to the dance with you."

"I know. It totally sucks, but I need to draw Dracula to the dance, and I don't want him to be scared off by having a Van Helsing there. Christopher will be there, but not obviously. Not as my date. It's part of the plan. So . . . I'll be going solo. Or as the third wheel to you and Mark."

"But you'd *rather* be going to the dance with Christopher."

I nodded. "He'll be there, though, with Kayla. Somewhere in the building. Waiting for Dracula. We're going to draw him to the theater and trap him there. How does this look?" I held up a tiny little minidress in black velvet.

"Pretty. Would show off your boobs."

"Hmm. What are you wearing again?"

"That ivory satin dress Bebe found for me. It's a slip dress. Sexy."

"*Cold*. You'll freeze your ass off."

"But I'll look good doing so."

"What's Mark wearing?"

"He's borrowing his older brother's suit, and he *promised* me he wouldn't let his mother near him with the razor before the dance. I'd like him to have some hair."

"Do you ever think you could maybe like him?"

"Mark?"

"Yeah, Mark."

"The Mark we do everything with. The Mark who can burp his entire way through the alphabet. The Mark who can't dance. The Mark who thinks a Notre Dame T-shirt is acceptable attire to any function?"

"Yes, that Mark. He's also the Mark who brought you flowers when Carl broke up with you. He sat up with you when you had mono and watched movies all night with you. He's the Mark who always helps us with homework. He's always there for us—always."

I took the black dress and two others and headed toward the fitting room.

"Actually," Mina said, "I do kind of think of him that way. When we were at the Underground dancing, and I was in his arms, I wondered for a minute what it would be like to kiss him. I mean, I know he's a little . . . dorky, but you know, Lucy . . . he is the sweetest guy I've ever known. I think I just always told myself you and he would one day end up married and live happily ever after with fifteen kids somewhere."

I started laughing. "Nah. I love Mark, but he's like my brother. His whole family is like my family. Even Jimmy the bug eater."

I took off my jeans and sweater and tried on the little black dress.

"Luce." Mina gasped. "You look beautiful."

I stared at myself in the mirror. I pulled my hair

off of my face, and for the first time I noticed how much like my mother I looked. With the neckline of the dress, though, I looked even more like Lucy Barrows, the first Lucy. I took an elastic from my purse and put my hair in a ponytail, which I loosened until my hair resembled the picture from the locket.

"You look like that picture you showed me," Mina said, her eyes wide. "Like her twin."

"I do, don't I?" I whispered.

It was as if I were really her. My ancestor. The girl who started all of this. Now I just needed to draw Dracula to me, so he could see me looking like her. I was making myself into vampire bait. I slid my hand down my neck. I didn't mind being bait—I wanted to slay Dracula. I just hoped to avoid being a midnight snack for him beforehand.

Chapter 26

I told my mom about you," Christopher said. We were lying on my bed—in clothes—making out and listening to a Coldplay CD.

"What did she say?"

He traced my face with his finger. "To be careful. But that if I felt for you like she felt for my father, then it was destiny."

Ophelia, I'd since learned from pictures and what Christopher told me, had long, blond, curly hair that she always tucked under a cap. Her eyes were pale blue, and she had reacted to Professor V's disappearance by spending days on the sea.

"Did you tell her about . . ." I still hadn't *quite* figured out a way to refer to my cat as his father.

"Dad?"

I nodded.

"No. I figure if we can take down Dracula, then we get my dad back to normal—and *then* I can tell her."

"Good thinking."

"She still loves him. I know she does."

"Well, my father still loves my mom, though lately I think he's gaga over Ms. Harris—the school shrink."

Christopher shook his head. "My mother has never talked of any other man except for my dad."

I tried to picture her out at sea, alone with the wind and the whales. It sounded sort of romantic.

"Lucy . . . ?"

"Yeah?"

He turned my face to look directly at him. "I think I'm falling for you."

"Me, too."

"You know, my mother and I spent a lot of my childhood on the water. I was homeschooled. I guess I grew up thinking that everyone lived alone and watched the whales. But after a while, I felt . . . I didn't know what I felt, but even when we came back to the mainland, I realized it was loneliness. Like half of me was empty, but I hadn't the first clue for how to look for what was missing. Does that make any sense?"

"Yeah."

"Then I saw a picture of your mom, and I started to understand what my dad felt for her. I know he loved my mom, but I think he felt like your mom understood him better than anyone. I thought maybe it was in my blood to long for one person. Like it was my destiny. Even if I didn't know who that person was just yet."

"I think my mother felt like your father was a part of her, too."

"Lucy . . . you're so pretty." He leaned in and kissed me again. His hand slipped up my shirt and under my bra. I was so thankful my father was cool about us being alone in my bedroom. It's that trust thing again.

We kissed some more. I touched his hair and wrapped a curl around my pinkie.

"You're all I think about, Lucy."

"You're all I think about."

"Well . . . actually, I also think about killing Dracula. If we get him, Lucy, we can live our lives in peace."

"I know."

"Have you been trying to draw him to you? To the dance?"

I nodded.

"What's that like?"

"It's exhausting. It's like I try to project part of me to him, and I keep saying, in my mind, over and over again, 'Come to me, come to me, come to me.'

While I'm doing it, I'm not even aware of anything else. Then, eventually, I'm so exhausted I have to stop. I'm usually all sweaty and feverish. Then I have to eat something and take a shower and then do something else with my mind, to sort of shake the evil out of me."

"I'm scared for you."

"I'm not as scared as I used to be," I said, and kissed him.

We lay on my bed until around eleven. Then I walked him downstairs to say good night.

Kayla was waiting for him, curled across the welcome mat. Professor V had scampered under the couch at the sight of Kayla, and wherever he was, he wasn't coming out.

"I won't let anything happen to you," Chris said to me.

"Don't worry. I used to feel confused and scared. Now I'm just angry."

"Kayla and I will be at the dance. You won't see us, but we'll be there. Be careful."

"I will."

He kissed me again and then he and Kayla got into his somewhat rusty Toyota and drove away.

No sooner had they pulled out of the driveway than Professor V came and leaped up into my arms.

"Hey, there, old cat," I whispered. "He sure is nice."

I went up to bed and read another entry from my mother.

> Dearest Lucy,
>
> A scholar once said to me, as I was researching Bram Stoker, that Stoker's book was about the dawn of feminism. I secretly laugh at this theory. I mean, if it is about feminism, it is only because the real inspirations for Mina and Lucy were, in fact, strong women before their time.
>
> I haven't written to you about Mina. She was Lucy Barrows's best friend, an actress also. But she was wealthy, and her father didn't let her indulge in this acting bug of hers. From all I could find out about her, she married, but she was never happy. Instead she spent years searching for Lucy Barrows, who, for all her friend knew, disappeared off the face of the earth.
>
> Mina always blamed Irving and Stoker for the disappearance of the young actress, but she was branded "hysterical." So much for feminism. She wrote a series of letters to Lucy,

never mailed, that were found among her possessions after her death.

I have always felt the burden of my mother and her mother and her grandmother. But to be honest, my daughter, I would rather fight a vampire than be repressed and suppressed by circumstances and society. I would rather die, as it appears I am going to, than to give up my strength as a woman. Lucy, never hide your strength. Never allow someone else to dictate what happens to you. Take and hold firm to your inner strength. Believe in yourself. These are the lessons to be learned from Lucy and Mina.

Love,
Mom

Chapter 27

Vic had been avoiding me ever since we broke up. We didn't have any classes together, so that made it easier for him not to see me. But getting Jude—and hopefully Seth—to the dance was important to our plan. We wanted to bring down as many Irvings as possible. So the morning of the dance, I called Vic's house. Jude answered.

"Hello?"

"Hi, Jude, this is Lucy. Is Vic there?"

"Yeah. He's getting ready to leave for this stupid dance—he's on some committee."

"I guess I'll see him tonight then."

"You're still going?"

"Yeah. What of it?"

"Nothing." I heard him call for Vic, who then got on the phone.

"What do you want?" he snapped.

"Nothing. It's just that we've been friends a long time, and I just wanted you to know that I'm still going to the dance, but I would really like it if we weren't enemies. Maybe you could save a dance for me."

"Maybe." He sounded sullen.

"See you later then, Vic."

I hung up and hoped I had at least intrigued Jude enough that he might come just to the dance. I hoped that what I believed was true—that killing Dracula would free them. Most especially I wanted Vic to go back to being Vic. I shuddered every time I thought about him eating bloody meat, or worse, being a real vampire and drinking blood.

I spent the day getting ready. Mina and I went for manicures and pedicures. She got her hair done in an updo. I used a diffuser when I blew mine dry so that my curls would sort of behave. Then I pulled it up in a way that looked like the photo.

I sprayed both of us liberally with vampire repellent, and then Mina went home to get dressed. Her parents were letting her and Mark use their limo and usual chauffeur for the special occasion. They would come get me. The dorky one without a date.

The day before, a package had arrived from UCLA. My godfather had made Mark his special cologne. I called Mark and he came to get it around four that afternoon. We smelled the cologne.

"It's no Polo," I said. "But it'll do."

"As long as I'm not smelling like you and Mina, I'm happy." He took the bottle from me.

"So . . . you seem pretty psyched to be going with Mina," I said.

He shrugged. "Yeah. You know . . . would it bother you if Mina and I . . ."

"Hooked up?"

"Yeah."

"No. I'd be really happy for you guys. I mean . . . you're my two best friends. I love you guys. Besides, I've always known behind your teasing each other that maybe you each kind of liked the other."

"Lucy, you and me . . . well, you're my best friend, and I don't want to screw that up. I won't go out with Mina if it means messing us all up somehow."

"Come on. How could I ever get mad at the boy I took baths with in preschool?"

He smiled, gave me a hug, and went home to get changed.

"Remember," I said as he walked out the door. "No haircut."

"Yeah. I know."

He shut my bedroom door, and I started fussing

with my makeup. A little before seven I came downstairs and did a twirl for my dad in his study.

"Well?"

"You look beautiful, Luce. I just wish I were sure
everything was going to be okay tonight."

"It will be." I looked him up and down. "You
look pretty handsome, too. Nice suit. I don't think
I've ever seen you wear one."

He smiled and ran his hands through his hair. He
looked nervous.

"Dad?"

"Hmm?"

"I just want you to know it's okay to . . . date
Ms. Harris."

"Oh." He flushed. "I . . . er . . . uh . . . okay.
Thanks. I . . . I don't know."

"Are you going to be okay? Leaving the house.
Doing all this."

"I think so. It's a big step. But I can't hide in here
forever."

A short time later the doorbell rang. Mark and
Mina were on my porch—looking great together.
Mark said, "This was on your doorstep." He held
out a corsage in a see-through plastic box. A card
was on top. The corsage was beautiful—six baby
roses in mauve, with a pale pink ribbon.

> *To my beautiful Lucy, my soul mate*
> *Love, Christopher*

"How sweet!" Mina squealed.

I put on the wrist corsage and smelled the flowers. I had butterflies in my stomach. So much depended on my using powers I wasn't so sure I had.

My father snapped a bunch of pictures. We said good-bye to him, and then climbed into the limo. Dad was going to come later with Ms. Harris.

In the limo we drank soda and squeezed one another's hands for good luck. This so had to work. I focused my mind.

Come to me.

Come to me.

Come to me.

Even as I drew him to me, I couldn't think about the plan. It was like I had two sides to my brain. I couldn't let Dracula see into my mind, see what we had in store for him.

Come to me.

Come to the theater.

In the theater we had laid a trap. We hoped that if we lured him there, with me so closely resembling the original Lucy, and in a setting not unlike the Lyceum Theatre, he would feel confused, or at least pause for a moment—and that was when we would strike.

The parking lot of Pacific Cedar High School was packed. The chauffeur dropped us off in front of the building. We climbed out and walked to the front doors. Mina looked like a model in her dress, but she was freezing, just like I told her she'd be. Mark wrapped an arm protectively around her. I wished Christopher had been with me so he could have done the same. The three of us fell in with the crowds of kids making their way into the gym.

"Wow," I said when we arrived at the dance. The place looked magical. The homecoming committee members were greeting people as they entered, and Vic was there. My stomach tightened.

"Like it?" Vic asked.

"You guys did a great job," I said—and meant it. The gym had been transformed into its theme—*A Midsummer Night's Dream*. They had decorated the walls with branches from trees, and strung white lights on all the branches and overhead. It was like walking into a fairy forest.

"Save a dance for me, Lucy," Vic said, a little sadly.

"I will."

We found a table. It was me, Mark, and Mina, along with some friends from our classes. There were three or four tables filled with Goth kids. They were dressed all in black—the girls wore Renaissance-looking dresses, or flowing black skirts with leather tops and black dog collars. Some of them had safety pins instead of earrings. It was a look. I could tell some were vampires.

"Mina, look." I elbowed her. Seth and Jude had slipped in with the crowds. Occasionally we glimpsed them. They stayed to the shadows, and their eyes were flat and hollow.

I kept glancing around to see if I saw Kayla or Christopher, but I didn't. I believed him, though, when he said he would be there somewhere. I had to have faith.

While we had been getting ready today, I knew Mr. Dobbs had been preparing for the showdown. Mr. Dobbs had filled the punch bowl and the food with garlic and sulfur syrup my father had gotten Uncle Jack to concoct. The ice was made with holy water—thank God for Mark's aunt, Sister Margaret. Vampires were going to be getting a stiff dose of food poisoning.

In the theater we had rigged a trap. We planned to open the trapdoor on the stage, and underneath it was a tub of holy water. I was to get Dracula to stand directly over the door, while Mark and Mina blinded him with a spotlight and pulled the lever to make the trapdoor open. Mr. Dobbs said that as powerful as Dracula was, the holy water wouldn't kill him. But we had buckets of garlic poison ready to dump down on him. If he was still alive after that, we would resort to a stake through his heart while he was sick and dying.

Around eight o'clock, Mina elbowed me. "There's your father," she whispered. Ms. Harris had picked him up. It had been so long since he drove a car, he didn't even have a valid license.

I was so proud of him for overcoming his fears. I rose from my chair and went over to my father. "Dance, Dad?"

"I have two left feet."

"That's okay."

He smiled at Carolyn, and then he took my hand. His were clammy. We moved out onto the dance floor.

"I'm really proud of you, Dad. Are you all right?"

"Yeah. I think so." We swayed to the music. "Which one is Mr. Dobbs?"

I jerked my head to the left. "That one over

there. He said to tell you and Uncle Jack thanks for the formula. Oh . . . and avoid the punch. It's loaded with garlic juice masked with honey. And there's garlic in the brownies. Stick with the crudite and the cheese platter."

My father smiled. "We just might pull this off."

"Mr. Dobbs has been perfecting some of these recipes for years."

Dad and I danced to a slow Beyoncé song. Then something fast came on.

"No chance of me dancing to this one, Luce."

"That's all right. Besides, Ms. Harris is over there. She's waiting for you." I stood on tiptoe and kissed his cheek. Then I went back to sit down.

Mark had his arm around Mina. She looked happy.

"So do you really think Dracula will show up?" Mina asked.

"Yup. I think having you and me both here is too tempting to resist."

I avoided the punch and munched on some celery with ranch dip. Vic came over to our table. He looked pale and sick.

"Something wrong?" I asked innocently enough.

"Yeah. I feel sick to my stomach. I swear it's something I ate."

"Why don't you have some punch? Maybe it will settle your stomach."

"I already did."

I surveyed the gym. At the vampire table—at least that's what I called it, because all of them appeared to sit together—they all were doubled over, heads in their hands.

I exchanged a look with Mr. Dobbs. He looked pretty pleased with himself.

Ms. Harris and my dad were heavy into conversation. Then I saw her look at her watch. She excused herself and went over to the deejay and took a microphone from him.

"Students . . ." she said, and waited for everyone to quiet down. "It's time to announce the homecoming court."

One by one she announced the names of the court. Several girls went up with their dates. Then two guys were called.

"And our next court member is Victor Irving."

My eyes widened.

"Come on," Vic said, and squeezed my hand. "Come up with me, Lucy. Please." He looked so pale, I felt bad, but I nodded yes and we joined the other court members. Ms. Harris announced three more names. Then she took an envelope from the assistant principal.

"Every student standing here deserves the honor of homecoming king or queen. We'll have two king and queen couples. When I announce your name, please go to the middle of the dance floor with your date for the first dance as king and queen."

The gym grew even quieter.

"The homecoming queen is . . . Elizabeth Martin."

I tried to avoid rolling my eyes. Elizabeth is one of those never-a-hair-out-of-place girls. She's just a little *too* perfect. She has a 4.0 grade point average and is on track to be class valedictorian.

Elizabeth was given a tiara and a sash, and her date was given a small crown.

"And the homecoming king is . . . Victor Irving, with his date Lucy Hellenberg."

Vic took me by the hand and led me onto the dance floor. I got a tiara and he got a sash and a crown. He put the sash on me, his face nearly green, and we prepared to dance.

At that precise moment, the double doors to the gym opened—the ones that led out to the fields. In strode Dracula. He was handsome and elegant, very tall, with dark eyes that were so intense. His hair was black and slicked back. His forehead was unlined. I could see his eyes darting around the gym looking for me. I could hear him in my head.

Tonight, you're mine.

I pulled away from Vic.

"I need to go."

He looked at me. "What's going on?"

"Vic . . . you don't have to be like your family."

He blinked slowly and looked like he wanted to say something. But I didn't have time. I ran from him and then from the gym. Mina and Mark were going to take a shortcut to the theater, and my dad and Mr. Dobbs would be hurrying there as well.

I ran out into the hall and made a right down a long, empty corridor. The school was creepy. Even though I could hear music from the gym, the halls echoed from my heels pounding, and they were dark and hushed.

Follow me, I urged Dracula in my mind.

I could feel him. I looked over my shoulder and he was, I swear, just five feet away from me. I had no idea how he could move that fast, but I was still too far from the theater. I ran faster.

Suddenly I felt myself being lifted off the

ground. I was smashed against a locker, but no one was touching me. He was hurling me with his mind.

Foolish girl. You're mine. You can't escape.

I was pinned against the locker as he took two steps toward me and bared his fangs. I felt anger. I mean, I was scared, but this was the vamp who got my mother sick, and for that I wanted him dead.

I shut my eyes and tried to use my mind. From somewhere in the pit of my stomach—in that place where I felt anger in my belly—I demanded, *Release me.*

I fell to the floor in a heap. I had done it! I had fought his power with my own. Excitement surged through me. My mother was right. I called up the power from my belly again and aimed my mind against him. I slammed his shoulder into a locker, and I heard him mutter, "Damn!"

I scrambled from the floor and started running again. I could feel his mind tugging on my dress, trying to stop me. I whirled around, my anger fiercer, and lifted him with my mind and dumped him to the floor.

Lucy, you're too young, too unpolished. I've been doing this for many lifetimes.

I was flung up to the ceiling and pressed against it. I stared down at the floor. Man, when he dropped me, this was going to hurt. My arms were pinned up to the ceiling too, leaving me unable to put them in front of me to break my fall.

He stood below me.

"I feel like a cat with a new *chew* toy." He waved his hand and I fell down, smashing my cheek into the cold linoleum floor. I felt like I had broken my arm, and I groaned.

I stood up slowly, moving my hurt arm and shoulder. It wasn't broken, but I was even angrier. I imagined, in my mind, punching him in the gut. Suddenly he was bent over and I felt his hot breath hit me as the air left his lungs, just as if I had really punched him in the stomach with all my might.

I turned and ran, feeling that the heel on my right shoe was broken. I raced toward the double doors that led into the theater. I ran down the middle aisle.

Ahhhh, blood sacrifice in the theater. What memories this conjures.

I ran up the steps and onto the big stage. Mark had taped an X where I was supposed to stand. He and Mina shone a single, flattering white light on me.

I am Lucy Barrows, I thought. *Come to me.*

Dracula stood right in front of the stage. "Your resemblance to her is uncanny."

204

I stared at him. He hadn't aged over time. Immortality bought with blood.

He levitated himself and stood near me.

"Lucy . . ." he whispered.

I looked toward the light board in the back of the theater. On cue, Mina and Mark shone the hottest, whitest light in the entire theater right in his eyes. He held his hand up. "It burns!"

I pushed him with my mind just a half step. My father, hidden from sight, pressed the lever, and the trapdoor opened. Dracula fell through and I heard a yell as his feet landed in holy water.

Mr. Dobbs and my father emerged from the curtains with buckets, ready to hurl them down the trap and cover him with garlic oil, but before they could do that, Dracula rose from beneath the stage, emerging from the hole of the trap door, his face clearly marked by pain, his very legs sizzling. Steam rose off his body from where the holy water touched him.

This wasn't good.

My father and Mr. Dobbs each threw their buckets of oil in Dracula's direction, but with his mind he deflected them, and the buckets simply fell to the ground.

This was doubly not good.

"Lucy, run!" Mr. Dobbs shouted.

I turned and ran down the steps. I would go back to the gym, in front of all those people. As I left the theater, I saw Dracula soaring, flying toward me. It reminded me of the time Mina's parents took us to New York City and we saw *Phantom of the Opera* where the phantom flew through the theater on special pulleys. Only in Dracula's case, it wasn't ropes and pulleys and tricks of the stage that helped him fly through the theater, just his own power.

I ran out into the hall and down toward the gym, all the while trying to hurl him against the walls. He was gaining on me, and I felt as if I were running through ice water. My legs were heavy, and a chill came over me. I heard my father, Mr. Dobbs, Mina, and Mark running down the hall, their footsteps echoing. I reached the doors to the gym, but I could barely move, not from the painlike pins and needles, but icy ones. With my last burst of energy, I crashed through the doors and back into the homecoming dance, falling to the floor in a heap.

But Dracula didn't follow. He disappeared, just fog and a shadow where he had been. My dad reached me and knelt and threw his arms around me.

"Oh, my God, but that was close." He kissed the top of my head and helped me to my feet. Everyone was staring at me. I felt my cheek. A streak of blood was there. Blood was smeared on my sash.

Then, without warning, a huge black wolf charged into the gym.

Everyone in the place started shrieking as the wolf paced in large circles, snarling and snapping its jaws. Saliva dripped on the ground. The food-poisoned vampires were, in fact, the only people not shrieking besides me and Mark and Mina . . . and Vic, who had come over to me and my dad.

"How come you're not afraid?" I asked Vic.

"Because screaming will only make things worse. Let's just quietly head to an exit. Back up slowly."

"No," I said, and stood my ground.

"What?"

"That's your grandfather, isn't it? That wolf. Or great-grandfather. And where are Jude and Seth?"

"I don't know." Vic grabbed a chair and held it out, as if to fend off the wolf if it came toward us.

The wolf came right at us, snarling even louder. My father and Mr. Dobbs stood between me and the wolf, which seemed only too eager to bite either of them. It rose up on its hind legs and bared its fangs. At that moment, though, Kayla bounded into the room.

All around us, chaos swirled. People were screaming, climbing over one another to escape. Someone tipped over the entire buffet table. The punch bowl crashed and broke into a thousand pieces.

Mina and Mark were hurling chairs at vampires.

My father and Mr. Dobbs were flinging silverware at Seth and Jude.

And Kayla attacked the black wolf.

The two of them now were snarling and growling in the center of the gym. Each would charge at the other, try to bite and claw, then retreat, pace and try again.

I looked around the room for Christopher. And then I heard the voice.

Lucy . . . I came here for you. Just as I came for your mother. You shall not defeat me.

The voice I had heard in my dreams. I said a silent prayer that Kayla could protect me.

I replied back to Dracula. *This time I'm strong enough and smart enough. This time you lose.*

The two wolves battled on. Blood spattered the walls. By now the police had come—someone must have dialed 911. I wondered what the 911 operator must have thought. Two wolves? A prank call?

Seth and Jude stood on the periphery, urging on

the black wolf. Most of the kids had left the gym and were standing outside in the cold.

Kayla yelped. I felt panic stir in my belly. She had to win. She just had to. Our whole plan was now contingent on the black wolf being defeated.

But Kayla limped and collapsed. Tears came to my eyes. One of the police officers shouted, "Stand back!" He fired his gun at the black wolf, but it didn't react and came barreling for me.

Then Christopher shouted, "Over here!" He stood in the doorway to the gym with what looked like an arrow in his hand.

The wolf turned its head and paused for just a second. In that fraction of time, Christopher hurled the arrow and pierced its side. I knew what the arrow was—one of his father's titanium daggers.

The black wolf yelped, growled, and fell over. Christopher went running over and jammed the dagger in deeper.

The two police officers yelled, "Get away from that thing; it could have rabies."

Little did they know that what it did have was far worse.

Christopher stood over the wolf as it died. Its carcass immediately shriveled.

"What the . . . ?" one of the cops said.

I stood there, frozen. Could we really have defeated him? For real this time?

Jude and Seth ran from the room. The rest of us stood there in stunned silence.

Christopher ran over to me and hugged me to him. "I'm so glad you're okay."

I kissed him . . . and then saw Vic's face.

"What's going on, Lucy? You played me?" He shook his head and started to walk out of the gym.

"I'll be right back," I whispered to Christopher, and went and caught up with Vic.

"You know about Seth and Jude, right?" I asked him. "You know about all of it."

He wouldn't look me in the eye.

"Vic," I demanded. "I didn't play you. I had to do this. Your family has vampire lineage. You don't have to go along with them, Vic. You could break the cycle."

I felt so certain with Dracula dead that Jude and Seth and Vic would realize they were free.

"You know," he said softly, "I thought I could turn out different. I thought what you and I had was . . . you know, real. But you planned this whole thing to get at my grandfather, to get at my family. We're not friends, Lucy. We're enemies now."

"Vic . . . what was I supposed to do? It's your family that's caused all this."

"But not *me*, Lucy. What you did . . . man, that was low. So watch your back. You may have won this round, but you won't win forever." He looked at me, and for the first time I saw a flash of red in his eyes. Red like that face at my window that night. Vampire eyes.

Vic stared at me. "Someday I'm going to be powerful, too. And no one will ever hurt me again." He turned his back on me and walked off into the night. In the distance I could make out Seth and Jude waiting for him. He'd made his choice. My heart sank. They weren't as powerful as Dracula, but I knew my battles weren't totally over. I hadn't freed them all. They were too much under the spell of Dracula. They had tasted the power of vampirism and liked it.

When I got back to everyone, the cops were trying to take statements. I think they finally gave up and called it a "wild animal incident." Then I saw Christopher.

Kayla was lying on her side, breathing hard. Her white coat was bloody. Christopher knelt next to her, petting her.

"You need to get away from it, son. That thing's a wild animal."

"She's my pet," Christopher said, a catch in his voice.

"I'm sorry, son. You want us to put her out of her misery?" one of the cops asked.

Christopher looked absolutely stricken. My father walked over and put a hand on his shoulder.

"You should let her go in peace."

Christopher shook his head. "She has to make it. She *has* to."

He got right down on the floor and looked into Kayla's eyes as she took her last breath. Then he put his face against her neck and quietly whispered good-bye.

"Is Ophelia still at sea?" my father asked.

Christopher nodded.

"Come back to our house, then. Come on."

"I need to take Kayla."

My father looked at the police.

"We need to take some reports. We'll release her body to you later," one officer said.

I walked to Christopher's side and rubbed his back. "I'm so sorry."

He grabbed my hand and squeezed it. Turning sadly, we all left.

Dad and Ms. Harris rode in one car. Mina and Mark went in the limo, and Christopher and I rode in his car.

"What a mess," I whispered.

He just nodded, too emotional to speak.

We drove away from the school and eventually arrived at my house.

"Oh, my God," I said as all the air left my lungs.

There, sitting on the steps, was Professor Van Helsing, just as my mother described him, an older version of Christopher, dashing, handsome, and strong.

We parked the car and Christopher climbed out.

"Dad?"

Professor Van Helsing nodded, walked toward the car, and grabbed us both in a fierce hug.

"I thought this day would never come," he said. He kissed Christopher on the head. "And Lucy." He winked at me.

"Yeah?"

"Thanks for the catnip."

The three of us laughed and waited for my dad to come home. Then all of us, and Ms. Harris, stayed up until the wee hours catching up. I can't say Ms. Harris understood everything—who could?—

but she knew something very weird went down in the gym.

Later, Christopher took me out on the porch and kissed me. "I love you, Luce."

"I love you, too."

Epilogue

The newspapers carried the story of the bizarre wolf fight in the Pacific Cedar gym. They interviewed animal experts and zookeepers, even went so far as to find a wolf expert in Alaska, but no one could explain what happened or why.

Amazingly, because of all the commotion, it didn't appear as though anyone at the dance had any clue as to what was really going on. No one saw any vampires, and there were only vague references to food poisoning at school. Principal Becker, after much discussion with Mr. Dobbs, seemed willing to chalk it all up to a full moon.

But a lot's happened since the homecoming dance.

Mina and Mark are pretty serious. Bebe has given Mark a total makeover. No more Notre Dame shirts for him. But he goes with it. He wears Dockers, polo shirts, cool sweaters, and some very nice antivampire cologne. Bebe treats him like a Ken doll, with Mina as her Barbie doll.

Mina, Mark, and I still do everything together at

school, and he's still giving me the answers in math and I'm still editing his term papers.

Mrs. Carnahan is pregnant again. Thank God Mark will be off at college before this one is too big. I mean, just how many kids can they fit in that house?

Jimmy . . . well, even though we killed Dracula, he's still a bug eater. He still picks his nose. He still refuses to shower. So maybe he wasn't controlled by Dracula after all. Maybe he's just gross. In fact, I'm willing to go on record as saying he is, in fact, just a prepubescent boy. Gross and smelly.

Professor V moved in with Ophelia and Christopher in their house by the sea. Time hasn't dimmed his and Ophelia's love for each other. He's making up for lost time, doing research, spending a lot of time with Christopher and Ophelia, learning about what he missed all those years. He still, Christopher says, keeps a picture of my mother on his desk. I think he feels sad that he wasn't able to protect her from the vampires. I am so grateful for Professor V, though. He and my father picked up where they left off. I can glimpse a different side of my father when they're together—the man he was when he and my mother were young and in love.

School update. Well, Mrs. Ruthen gave me a

C-minus for my final grade. I officially passed Ruthless's class. If I never see another hypotenuse triangle, it'll be too soon. I still hate her. I still think she's evil. And if I ever spot fangs, I'll know why.

Vic . . . well, Vic hates me. He spread a rumor that I was a two-timer. Then he took to just staring me down. He despises me, and he's tighter than ever with Jude and Seth. The three of them go downtown a lot. They dress Goth, and they look angry all the time. I think Vic's turned—he's a vampire. He's been officially added to Mr. Dobbs's vampire organizational chart. In fact, I joke that he's head of the vampire union. But Mr. Dobbs says it'll be a long while before Jude and Seth and Vic are as strong as Dracula was—and for now they're too afraid of me to do anything more than try to psyche me out.

Mr. Dobbs gave me an A. But I earned it. I wrote a great term paper on Bram Stoker, complete with lots of research and footnotes. But I could have just written about my mom and grandmother and great-grandmother. I could have written about the powerful women in our family.

Ms. Harris—Carolyn—is dating my dad. This is beyond dorky. I mean . . . who wants their father to date a teacher from school? Let alone the school shrink. But he's happy. We still have all the locks on our house, but we also go out to eat now, and he remembers to make a sandwich for lunch most days, and he even cooks from time to time.

Christopher and I are still going strong. We'll fight the vampires together. He's my other half. I love him so much it hurts in a way. I love him, love him, love him.

I've read through the diary I inherited a few times now, page for page, word for word. I understand that even if you're afraid of something, you still have to stand up for what's right. Every time I see my mother's handwriting, I feel like I have a part of her. I hear her voice, and I can picture her in my mind. She's not so far away and distant anymore.

I have been working on developing my powers. I don't ever want to use them for evil—just good. Just fighting the undead. My mother was right . . . I'm stronger than I ever could have imagined. I once thought about using my mind-speak to cheat on my math test and get the answers from Mark, but I decided not to. I use it to fight vampires—that's it. And occasionally to levitate. I mean, that's pretty cool, right?

Most of all, I got my happy ending. I'm still the girl who lives in the Munsters' house. I'm still the girl with the Chia Pet hair and the father who's a bit eccentric. I'm still the motherless girl who was always different.

But now I've got my happy ending. I've got Christopher and Professor V. I've got my father and friends. Okay, so I keep a lot of garlic around, and there are crucifixes everywhere in my house—including the shower stall—but I'm Lucy and I'm in love. And high school may still suck . . . but it doesn't bite anymore.

Liza Conrad is also the author of *Rock My World,* as well as the author of the upcoming *Poker Diaries.* She lives in South Florida with her family and pets, and she *loves* a good scary movie, as well as old vampire movies. In her free time she enjoys playing poker, going to the beach, listening to music, and going to her favorite sushi restaurant. She can be reached at her Web site at www.lizaconrad.com.

If you liked *High School Bites*,
you'll love the next book
from Liza Conrad

THE POKER DIARIES

Coming from NAL Jam in March 2007

Read on for a sneak peek....

You know that ad campaign, "What happens in Vegas stays in Vegas"? I'm living proof that's not quite true.

My parents met on a New York-to-Los Angeles flight fifteen years and nine months or so ago. My mother, a museum curator, was going to view the private art collection of some rich dead guy. My father was going to play in an illegal poker tournament, though he didn't tell her that. He also didn't tell her about the outstanding warrant for his arrest in New Jersey, or that his nickname was Blackjack.

They were flying first class and, at least how Dad tells it, they were drinking a lot of free champagne. By the time they landed, they got the bright idea to tell my father's waiting limo driver to take them to elope in Las Vegas. Needless to say, more champagne was waiting in the back of the limo. By the time they realized this was all a very, very bad idea, my mother had the flu. Then she told herself it was an ulcer from too much stress at her job. And then, when she couldn't lie to herself anymore, she took a pregnancy test. I am a souvenir from the one, lone impetuous act my mother has ever done in her life. A souvenir of Vegas. And I didn't stay in Vegas. Nope, I came along nine months later back in New York. So much for that slogan.

I give my parents credit. They tried to work it out for a year. My father dressed up in tuxedos and went to museum exhibit openings, even though his idea of art is that painting of the dogs playing poker.

My mother, for her part, tried to learn that a flush beats a straight. She let my father's buddies come to our Central Park West apartment for poker night once a week—even though she cringed at the cigar smoke and foul language. But even that was a disaster because the first time my dad asked her to make some snacks for his poker night, he was thinking peanuts and chips and maybe a six-foot-long sub with extra salami, and she served caviar with toast points and endive lettuce with lobster salad.

So, when I was a couple of months old, my parents got divorced, but in all these years they've never, ever said a bad word about the other one. I live with my mom on the upper east side of Manhattan during the week, and every other weekend, and for a month each summer, I go off with my dad to his neighbor-hood in Clinton—what used to be called Hell's Kitchen—and sometimes to Atlantic City or Las Vegas.

I love both my parents. When I was little, my mom never let me read the back of the cereal box during breakfast. Instead, she'd open up a big, glossy coffee-table art book to a page on Degas, or Michelangelo, or some other artist, and she would teach me. She'd say, "Lulu, look how the Flemish painters' portraits look almost like photographs." Or she'd tell me about Goya, her favorite painter of all, and of his "mad" period when he supposedly painted himself out of insanity. She brought me to museums and galleries, and we took trips to places like Venice and Florence.

When I would visit my dad, he'd teach me how to shuffle cards, or how to pick a horse at the race-track in Belmont. He taught me how to fill out the box scores at Yankees games. He'd take me to jazz clubs and to boxing gyms. I was even with him when he got my name tattooed on his right bicep, right below my mom's name.

But as cool as all this might sound, and as lucky as I am that my parents are divorced but still really like each other, I knew that one day my downtown world with Dad would come colliding into my up-town world with Mom. Which was why I tried to tell her that dating New York City's most eligible bachelor was a very bad idea. Almost as bad as elop-ing with my father to Las Vegas. But my mother didn't listen to me, which was why I was now "this close" to calling the mayor of New York my new stepdad. And why my life got completely and totally out of control.

I'm Lulu King, and my life is *The Poker Diaries*.